"What do you think you're playing at?"

Adam raised a lazy eyebrow. "Payment for services rendered," he replied. "Every wife's entitled to a cut...unless, of course, you'd like payment in kind?"

"You really must be joking," Denise spat. "I wouldn't want you if you were the last man on earth!"

"No?" Adam moved, and with a lightning flick of an arm he'd snared Denise. "Are you sure?" he whispered, locking his gaze onto hers.

Margaret Callaghan was born in Liverpool, England, in 1953. She was brought up and educated in the nearby market town of Ormskirk, Lancashire, famed for its gingerbread and its unusual parish church boasting both steeple and tower. Margaret is married with one daughter, Laura, and has lived close to beautiful Cannock Chase in Staffordshire for several years. She currently teaches English at a West Bromich comprehensive school. Her loves include French wine, French food, French holidays, and, of course, in true romance tradition, husband, Rob.

Reluctant
Charade
Margaret Callaghan

Harlequin Books

TORONTO • NEW YORK • LONDON
AMSTERDAM • PARIS • SYDNEY • HAMBURG
STOCKHOLM • ATHENS • TOKYO • MILAN
MADRID • WARSAW • BUDAPEST • AUCKLAND

ISBN 0-373-17269-9

RELUCTANT CHARADE

First North American Publication 1996.

Copyright © 1995 by Margaret Callaghan.

CHAPTER ONE

'WHERE is she?'

'I don't know.'

'You're lying!'

'No!' Denise backed away as Adam crossed the room, the thrill of fear gripping her. It was always the same. Her legs would turn to jelly at the mention of his name, and a fleeting glance from jet-black eyes was enough to make her blood boil. Adam Walker barely noticed her existence yet managed to set her emotions churning. Alone—and the focus of attention for once—Denise felt faint.

'Where is she?' he repeated almost softly, halting in front of her. He folded his arms, the gesture casual yet threatening, and black eyes pinned hers with a silent, simmering menace. A single eyebrow rose. 'Well?'

Denise went weak, the panic rising in her throat, threatening to choke her, Jen's petulant words echoing in her mind. . .

'It's just not fair,' she'd sulkily declared, make-up for once neglected. 'How can he be so selfish? Some ghastly ancient relative decides to pay a visit and my career's forgotten.'

'But only for a week or two,' Denise had tried to soothe her, finding space to sit on the clothes-strewn

bed. As usual, Jen's room had resembled a bomb-
site and Denise had felt a spurt of irritation. Jen
would sail out with never a backward glance and
Denise would be left with the chaos. Still, anger
wouldn't help, she was all too aware, and, focusing
her gaze on her cousin's stormy face, she had tried
a sympathetic smile. 'His grandmother's ill, Jen,'
she'd softly reminded her. 'And Adam's all she's
got. He's not asking much, not really.'

'Hah!' Blue eyes had turned instantly scornful. 'I
might have known you'd side with Adam. Don't
think I haven't noticed how my mousy little cousin
blushes so sweetly whenever he's around. But you're
wasting your time,' Jen had tagged on cruelly.
'Adam has eyes for me and me alone, and that's the
way it's staying.'

'So you'll pass up the Italian trip?' Denise had
tried to probe, swallowing the bitter taste of pain.
Jen didn't mean to be cruel, was simply annoyed
that her handsome fiancé was digging in his heels.
Yet Adam did have a point, Denise acknowledged
fairly. They *had* just got engaged, his grandmother's
visit planned to coincide with the party.

'Wrong, Denise! This assignment's the chance of
a lifetime, and if Adam can't see it I'll just have to
teach him a lesson.'

'Rather you than me,' Denise had warned, but
Jen had been dismissive.

'I know Adam. He'll come round. And as for the
party——' She'd paused, shoulders lifting carelessly,
casually, her whole expression mocking. 'It will

keep. It will have to, since I'll be halfway across Europe earning all that lovely money.' And, clearly deciding the matter was settled, she turned her back, generous lips pouting in the glass as she double-checked the shine.

Denise had gone cold. How selfish she sounded, selfish and uncaring, and the words slipped out before she could think. 'Money isn't everything,' she'd coolly reminded Jen. But criticising Jen was never wise.

Her cousin's face changed like the wind. 'Don't be so naïve,' she'd snapped. '*You* might be happy earning a pittance, but I'm not. Money's my security. *This* is my security,' she'd pointedly added, granting her reflection an approving smile. 'So Adam and his family will just have to wait. Jenny Elliot has better things to do than pander to an invalid. . .'

Logging the set of Adam's finely chiselled jaw now, Denise turned a whiter shade of pale. She hoped, she really did hope, that Jen knew what she was doing.

'Well?'

'Well, what?' Denise stalled, inwardly flinching at the fury in his eyes.

'Have you got a brain, Denise Elliot?' he tossed out coldly. 'Did the good lord endow you with some sense? Because if He didn't, heaven help you when I take this place apart. And that's exactly what I'll do if I don't get an answer—understand?'

She nodded, a nervous tongue sweeping dry lips,

the gesture unwittingly provocative, the kind of
thing that Jenny could use to devastating effect;
and, watching her, Adam's mouth tightened.

'You know,' he murmured evenly, almost confidentially, 'I hadn't realised how alike the two of you
are. Similar height, similar build.' Black eyes narrowed as they travelled the length of her, appraising,
assessing, lingering on the swell of breast beneath
the dusty blouse. 'A size bigger, maybe, an inch or
two shorter. The hair isn't right,' he carelessly
pronounced. 'Too long, too staid, too—*mousy*,' he
explained as Denise silently seethed. 'But it's all
there. And, in that case, your empty-headed cousin
might well have saved her pretty neck.' He smiled
grimly. 'But first we'll check the house. Knowing
Jen, this could be her idea of a game.'

'What are you doing?' Denise cried as he grabbed
her wrist and set off down the hall.

Adam ignored her, flinging open doors, pausing
for the briefest of moments to scan room after room
after room rapidly, a bewildered Denise half stumbling in his wake. In a matter of minutes he'd
completed the ground-floor survey and, darting her
a single withering glance, headed for the stairs.

'Adam!' She squirmed but Adam wasn't listening—leastways, not the Adam she was used to. That
he was ruthless in business she was all too aware,
but she'd never seen this side of him before. Had
Jenny? she fleetingly wondered, but the thought was
forgotten when they reached the first door. 'But this
is my room,' she objected automatically.

And still he didn't speak, dropping her hand like a lump of cold dough as he spied the walk-in wardrobes. In four long strides he was there, pushing clothes aside and peering into dark interiors, a furious Denise abandoned on the threshold. The last door slammed shut with unexpected vehemence.

'Satisfied?' she murmured sweetly as Adam drew level. 'She isn't here. I haven't seen her all day. As far as I knew, Jen was with you, getting things sorted for the party of the year. Don't tell me she's stood you up?' she enquired in a voice dripping poison.

A dull flush darkened his cheeks and Denise shrank against the woodwork as Adam pushed past, the contact brief but searing. Unnerved, she stood for a while, unconsciously massaging the wrist his fingers had bruised before creeping down the hall and into the room he'd deliberately left till last—Jenny's room. Lavishly decorated, sumptuously appealing—and empty.

'Well?' she couldn't resist goading. 'Happy now? Of course there's no need to ask if you've checked the shower-room, the dressing-room and underneath the bed. A man like you——' She broke off as he spun round, eyes twin pools of hate.

'Get your coat,' he ordered frigidly, the vicious gaze whipping her. 'And make it snappy. I haven't time to waste.'

'Why?' she asked, instantly wary. 'I'm not going anywhere.'

'No?' he queried silkily. 'Dear me.' He folded his

arms, leaning back against the wall, unconcealed amusement playing about the corners of his mouth. 'Didn't the ever-thoughtful Jenny issue an invitation?'

'As a matter of fact, Mr Know-It-All Walker,' Denise replied pertly, 'she did. It just so happens I turned it down.'

'And it just so happens, Miss Self-Assured Elliot, that the invitation stands. And, unlike Jen, I refuse to take no for an answer.' He smiled, black eyes holding hers, daring her to contradict.

Denise shrugged. Adam was wrong. She wasn't going. She didn't even like parties, and besides she had too much to do. And if Jenny didn't mind, why should Adam object? He was barely aware of her existence at the best of times, and with two hundred guests expected to wine and dine and dance the night away one insignificant poor relation surely wouldn't be missed. An absentee fiancée, though, was something else. Denise half smiled. She was almost tempted to change her mind, see how the arrogant Adam Walker wriggled out of that.

He must have caught the gist of her amusement for he moved suddenly, like a cat on the prowl, and had crossed the room before she could react. Reaching out, he gripped her shoulders, spinning her round to face the glass, his reflected gaze urgently compelling.

'Take a good look,' he entreated silkily, his breath a warm flutter on her neck. 'Take a good look and tell me what you see.'

Discarded clothes still covered Jen's bed and Denise watched warily as Adam snatched a dress, pinning it against her, long, slender fingers branding her flesh.

'Well?' he prompted softly. 'Beginning to get the picture? Beginning to see why you've had a change of heart? Ah, yes! I thought you might,' he drawled as colour swamped her cheeks. 'After all, education sharpens the mind, and with a first-class degree. . . Now, if you'd turned your talents to the theatre,' he tagged on provokingly, 'it would have paved the way for the role you're about to play. Miss Elliot,' he solemnly informed her reflection, 'meet the new Miss Elliot.'

'You're mad! You'll never pull it off. I'm nothing like Jen——'

'Wrong, Denise! You're uncannily alike. All that's needed is a subtle change of style. The right make-up, the right hair, the right dress——'

'And the fastest crash diet the world has ever seen. Or doesn't a stone and a half of extra flesh count?' she jeered. 'It would take a magic wand, and even the powerful Adam Walker would have trouble waving that.'

'Would I?' he challenged softly.

There was a long, long pause, tension quivering on the air, and Denise held her breath, tracing the figures in the smoked-glass panel, a muted effect, an uncanny effect, heightened by the dress held against her. She was shockingly aware of the hands on her shoulders, of the handsome face unnervingly close to hers. Tall, slim, yet powerfully built, he framed her body exactly, and, achingly used to seeing him with Jen, she could almost believe that it was Jenny's face, Jenny's figure in the glass. Almost. Oh, yes, the dress was real enough, but everything else paled in comparison. Denise smiled grimly. The idea was ludicrous.

'So,' Adam informed her coolly. 'It's settled.'

'Oh, no! Masquerade as Jen to save your face? No chance! If you need a fiancée, Adam, hire a professional. I'm staying put.'

'Wrong again. My grandmother's here to meet the blushing bride, and she's already seen a photograph of Jen.' He shrugged. 'It's you—or nothing. And, if the party's off, your ambitious cousin will have waved goodbye to that glorious, glittering future.' There was a pause, just long enough for the poison to take, for the softly spoken words to explode in her mind. 'She couldn't exactly blame you, Denise,' he pointed out slyly. 'But you do have the means to change my mind. And since Jen's family took you in. . .'

Denise went cold. How dared he? How dared he remind her? They'd been raised almost as sisters, though Denise had never shaken off the 'poor relation' tag, and with her aunt and uncle no longer alive it was just Jenny and Denise now. And Jenny—beautiful, spoiled, thoughtless Jen—had jetted off to Milan, supremely sure that Adam would understand.

He was bluffing, of course, she swiftly reassured

herself. Adam wouldn't hurt Jen for the world. But if he chose to rock the boat, she realised sickly, Jen would lose the only thing she craved—the security of money. Adam smiled in the glass. She was cornered and he knew it.

'I'll wait downstairs,' he murmured easily. 'You've five minutes to make up your mind. And, Denise, don't bother packing. You're simply perfect as you are. Five minutes,' he repeated softly. 'And not a minute more.'

I still think you're mad,' she muttered in the car.

She'd taken him at his word, grabbing coat and bag and sauntering down as the deadline was expiring, aware from the set of his mouth that he'd almost given up. Denise had swallowed a smile. Rich and handsome he might be, and clearly used to getting his own way, but Denise was an unknown quantity. She couldn't be bought and she couldn't be charmed, and to a man like Adam it must be galling—almost as galling as an absentee bride on the eve of the wedding. Denise scowled. She would wring Jenny's neck, given half a chance, though she wouldn't have minded betting that when her feckless cousin did arrive back she'd be in for one hell of a grilling.

'Maybe,' Adam acknowledged lightly. 'But we've twenty-four hours to play with, and in the meantime the ins and outs of this little problem are nothing but a mild irritation.'

Mild irritation? Jen? Denise almost choked. A

lethal dose of nettle-rash would be nearer the mark.
Then Adam's words sank in. Twenty-four hours.
Plenty of time to contact Jen and put her in the
picture. She'd book the first plane home, Denise
reassured herself, and, in that case, why not simply
humour Adam?

'So,' she enquired, visibly brightening, 'what's the
plan? I might fool a sick old lady, Adam, but
someone's bound to give the game away, leaving
you looking stupid.'

'Wishful thinking?' he challenged, with a lazy,
mocking smile. 'It couldn't be simpler. I ring a few
friends and tell them the truth—Jen's had to work;
you're standing in.' He shrugged. 'Word gets
around. End of problem.'

'Ah, yes. End of problem—until someone has one
drink too many and lets my name slip. Wriggle out
of that one, sir—if you can.'

'I'll think of something, oh, ye of little faith,' he
drawled. 'Just you wait and see.'

Denise hid a smile. She was almost looking forward to it—except she wouldn't be around to join
in the charade. It wasn't going to happen. Jen
wouldn't allow it. And she snuggled down into the
soft leather upholstery, aware of Adam's long,
tapering fingers on the wheel. M1, she idly noted,
and several minutes passed before the meaning of
that sank in.

'Where are we going?' she demanded, jerking
bolt upright. 'I thought the party was at your place.'

'So it is,' he agreed, with another mocking smile.

'But I've some business to see to, and where I go, you go. Since Jen's disappeared, you're my security.'

'So I gathered,' she acknowledged coolly. 'But I can be trusted, Adam, and once I've given my word, I keep it.'

'The word of an Elliot,' he pronounced cruelly, 'isn't worth the paper it's written on. Like it or not, you're staying with me.'

'That should be cosy,' she found herself deriding. 'So where *are* we going, assuming I'm allowed to know?'

'London. The house is full of caterers and staff setting up the party, so we're better off in Town. Besides——' he paused, darting her a calculated, sideways glance '—I've a magic wand to wave, remember? The new Miss Elliot,' he explained enigmatically, 'is about to go shopping.'

Only Adam's idea of shopping, she discovered belatedly, matched the rest of his lifestyle—complete and utter extravagance.

'Oh, no!' Denise stopped dead on the broad expanse of pavement outside an exclusive fashion house. 'A dress for the party is one thing, Adam, but a whole new wardrobe?' She shook her head emphatically. 'It's a waste of money.'

'My money,' he reminded her curtly. 'And no one, but no one, tells me how to spend it.'

Grey eyes turned instantly flinty. 'I'm not Jenny,' she snapped. 'I'm not some empty-headed bimbo

you can buy with furs and fripperies. I'm me—
Denise Elliot. Country Cousin maybe, poor relation
maybe, but I've never been short on pride. *I* buy
my clothes and *I* decide what I'm wearing.'

'Wrong!' he contradicted coldly, his whole
expression tightening. 'What you did last week is
your concern, but as long as Jenny's absent you're
wearing her shoes whether you like it or not. You'll
look like Jen, act like Jen, dress like Jen——'

'And when the clock strikes midnight I'll crawl
into your bed—hey, Adam?' she couldn't resist
needling.

The pause was electric, and Denise held her
breath, shockingly aware of the tension in the air,
of the silence screaming between them. Black eyes
narrowed, undercurrents swirling in treacherous
lagoons, and as the busy London street swam dizzily
out of focus Adam smiled.

'Now there's an idea,' he conceded dangerously.
'Why didn't I think of that?'

Colour flooded her cheeks. Oh, yes, she jeered
silently. She could see it now. The handsome Adam
Walker, one of the richest men in the world, making
love to mousy little her. Beautiful women had
swooned at his feet in droves and Adam had taken
his pick, rarely being seen with the same one twice—
until Jen came along that was. Jen. Breathtakingly
beautiful, ruthlessly determined—and shrewd
enough to hold herself aloof. And against all the
odds she'd hooked him, hooked the man whose
smouldering eyes now travelled Denise's body in the

most provocative way. He was playing with her, she realised painfully. And there wasn't a thing she could do to stop him—not without destroying Jen's dream.

'Very well,' she murmured coolly, breaking the silence but ignoring the goad. 'We go shopping; you foot the bill. But I'm warning you, Adam, choose something outrageous and the moment I'm alone all those highly expensive clothes turn into a heap of worthless rags.'

'For a girl with a social conscience, Denise, you're surprisingly free and easy with other people's cash.'

'Only yours,' she retorted fiercely, her chin snapping up in defiance. 'And what the hell do you know about my feelings?'

'More than you'd imagine,' he replied, an unfathomable emotion in those dark, brooding eyes.

Denise dropped her gaze as the pain rippled through her. Jen, she realised bitterly. She never missed a chance to tease, and had clearly informed her handsome fiancé of her cousin's 'schoolgirl crush'. That she was twenty-two didn't count. She'd never been at ease with the opposite sex, and though there had been men—boys, she acknowledged scornfully—from her university days, none had caused the fierce reaction that Adam seemed to provoke. And Jen, of course, had simply had to notice. Denise smothered a sigh. Jen didn't mean to be cruel, but sometimes, just sometimes, Denise wished that her early years hadn't been spent sharing a home with her beautiful, generous, but ever-thoughtless cousin.

Twenty-four hours, she consoled herself, marching rigidly inside. And not a minute more.

It was quite an experience, a private showing, she discovered at once, lips twisting in silent disapproval. The fashion house screamed money in a genteel, understated way: soft lights, background music, the wall to wall luxury of carpets and furnishings. But, as dress after dress was skilfully paraded and Denise was given no say, her mind slipped sideways, the movement and colour just a meaningless blur as her troubled thoughts turned to Jen and the need to persuade her cousin to take the first plane home.

'The green or the blue?' a voice prompted silkily, dragging her rudely back to the present.

She jumped, colour flooding her cheeks. 'The green or the blue what?' she enquired warily, eyes sweeping the now empty rostrum.

'Would it matter?' Adam enquired deceptively mildly. 'Shoes, dress, hat? Bra, pants, petticoat? A herd of tutu-clad hippos would have made the same impact.' His voice changed, the sugar coating melting into venom. 'Start acting, my dear,' he niggled pointedly. 'Pay attention. You're supposed to be in love, remember—with me. Smile, simper, glow; send long, loving glances my way—and show the tiniest bit of interest in your trousseau,' he entreated frigidly.

'Why?' Denise demanded, darting eyes checking

that they couldn't be overheard. 'Why the hell should I? *You're* paying the bill, you're choosing the clothes—and I clearly can't be trusted to select my own tights. What's the matter?' she went on, throwing caution to the winds. 'Is the ego in need of a feed?' she scorned. 'Not getting all the love and attention it doubtless takes for granted? Perhaps we'd better call it a day——'

'Not a hope in hell,' he growled. 'We have ourselves a deal. Two weeks of your time. And think what you'll be doing—helping Jen, helping me, not to mention a sick old lady. You couldn't walk away from that, could you, Denise?' he pointedly reminded her. 'Unless,' he tossed out bitterly, 'I really have misjudged you.'

Denise smiled. 'You know, you might just be right,' she informed him sweetly. 'And you might just find out the hard way.'

'Meaning?' Black eyes hardened, narrowed, pinned her with their steely gaze, and Denise felt an unexpected twinge of fear.

'You're a bully, Adam Walker,' she told him coolly. 'Jen isn't here so someone else must play the starry-eyed lover, and who better than good old Denise, who can easily drop what she's doing and fit in with everyone else's plans? Except that underneath this calm exterior could beat a heart as cold and hard as nails. And when I leave you in the lurch——'

'Not me, Denise, Jenny—remember?'

'Ah, yes!' she acknowledged bitterly. 'How could

I forget the blackmail? Denise plays ball or Jen's made to pay the price.'

'Exactly! I couldn't have put it better myself.' He smiled, oh, so confident, and Denise felt the anger surge.

'Come off it, Adam,' she derided coolly. 'Who are you trying to kid? Ruin the woman you love just to hit back at me? You wouldn't dare.'

'Wouldn't I?' he challenged softly.

Denise smiled grimly. 'No,' she informed him scathingly, sickly aware that she couldn't be sure. He was a proud man and Jen had hurt him, and the need to hit back in turn might just gain the upper hand. 'It's an empty threat, and don't think I don't know it. You're bluffing.'

'Am I?' He smiled again, the supreme confidence galling, and as Denise visibly scowled Adam spread his hands. 'Well, if you say so,' he sneeringly allowed.

'I do,' she snapped, eyes daggers of hate. 'And sooner or later I'll prove it.'

The mocking smile broadened, but the expression in his eyes was enough to freeze the blood in her veins. 'Go ahead, Denise,' he goaded carelessly. 'If you dare. It's my bet that you haven't got the nerve.'

'No?' It was Denise's turn to sneer. 'Well, you would think that, wouldn't you, Adam? Which is why you'll lose.'

'The powerful Adam Walker against a slip of a girl?' Adam almost laughed. 'And how do you work that out?'

'You'll see,' Denise insisted, itching to wipe the knowing expression from the much too handsome face and, instead of leaving well alone, allowing the thought to goad her. 'Because I can pick my moment, Adam. I can watch and wait, and when you've dropped your guard, when you're least expecting it, well——' She shrugged casually, provokingly, off-handedly. 'By then, it will be much, much too late.'

He swore lightly under his breath, thunder and lightning blasting his features, and Denise shrank away, backing into the corner of the sumptuous settee, the reaction futile as strong arms reached out, fastening round her shoulders, the heat spreading out from harsh points of contact.

'No one threatens me, Denise,' Adam crooned contemptuously, pulling her towards him. 'No one. I want your help, I need your help and, like it or not, you'll give it—willingly, happily or as grudgingly as you choose, as long as the rest of the world is fooled. And believe me, madam, it had better be good.' He shook her roughly. 'Are you listening?' he demanded frigidly, that angry face unnervingly close. 'You're mine—for the next fourteen days. You'll smile, you'll glow, you'll flirt; you'll kiss and be kissed; you'll live and breathe the role Jen has forced you into. And when it's over you can crawl back into your shell and sleep for the rest of your life, if that's what you want. You'll be free—as long as Kate goes home happy.'

'Kate?' she murmured, more stunned than angry,

the hands on her shoulders causing chaos in her mind.

'My grandmother. The reason you're here—the *only* reason you're here—and don't you forget it.' He released her abruptly and Denise slumped awkwardly into the corner, blinking back the tears. 'I'll be back,' Adam hissed, standing up and towering above her, black eyes raining scorn, 'when I've made some phone calls. In the meantime, you've got what you've been angling for. You're on your own, Denise. Choose wisely, won't you?'

Tears welled afresh as Adam strode away, and Denise sniffed loudly into the silence, jumping in alarm as a diplomatic cough reached her ears. With super-human effort she spun round, forcing a smile for the hovering Claud.

'That only leaves the cocktail dresses,' he murmured sympathetically. '*Monsieur* didn't seem to have a preference. Perhaps we could show you our latest designs. . .?'

Denise nodded, grateful for the precious few moments he gave her alone, for the welcome cup of coffee that appeared at her side. For two pins she'd walk out now, out of Adam's life and out of Jenny's too, she realised starkly. She'd be losing a lot, but material things didn't count. And Adam was wrong. She could cope by herself, find a studio somewhere else. She was almost established, was beginning to make a name for her distinctive hand-thrown pottery, and as long as she made enough to pay the rent and cover the basics she would be content. She *could* cope, she decided fiercely, but there would be a price—Jen. Hurt, angry, bewildered, and sure to blame Denise.

Twenty-four hours, she silently repeated, refusing to believe that it could be any longer. But she'd need to contact Jen—and soon.

He was less than an hour. The powerful form filled the doorway, drawing her gaze, and as Denise's wayward body reacted to the sight a memory stirred. Smile? Simper? Glow? Boy, would she show Adam! And she sailed across before she could change her mind.

'Darling,' she gushed, launching herself into his stunned embrace. 'You won't believe the dress I've chosen for the party. It's out of this world,' she revealed gleefully, raising her face for a kiss and registering the shock in jet-black eyes. And as his lips brushed hers, briefly, searingly, unnervingly, she added softly, provokingly, with the merest hint of defiance, 'Just like the price. But I'm worth every penny, hey, Adam?'

'You'd better be,' he agreed pleasantly, the velvet tone threaded with iron. 'Believe me, Denise, you'd better be.'

He didn't speak at all as the lift zoomed down to the basement and Denise stole a glance at the uncompromising profile. It wasn't reassuring. His mouth was set grimly, the aquiline nose eagle-like and cruel. An easy man to like when he turned on the charm, but Denise could imagine how he'd deal with opposition. He had a ruthless reputation in the City—hard-headed, hard-hearted. He'd fought his way from the bottom to the top, arriving from the States with a few thousand pounds, investing, rein-vesting, seeking out a rival's weakness and turning countless foundering companies round as he carved out an empire—Adam Walker's empire. And only a fool would choose to forget that what Adam Walker wanted, Adam Walker took—by fair means or foul. Denise went cold. And only a fool, she told herself belatedly, would choose to cross him. She shivered, though the afternoon was warm. She wouldn't want to be in Jen's shoes when she did come home, but in the meantime Denise was the one heading for that fall.

He led her to the car, a dark, sleek Alfa Romeo that purred like a panther on an open road. 'Ah, well,' she muttered under her breath, bracing herself for the short, tense journey to the hotel—Adam's hotel, she supposed idly. 'Here goes.'

Only she was wrong. Adam turned towards her instead, and released the seat-belt she'd nervously slotted into place. A terrible thought ran through her mind, the chill-thrill of premonition.

'What are you doing?' she demanded as long, tapering fingers closed about her shoulders, drawing her nearer and nearer to that inscrutable face, that forceful body, that much too masculine form. The panic was rising in her voice. 'Adam! What on earth are you doing?'

'Can't you guess?' he entreated silkily, pinning

her fast with the force of his gaze, the strange compulsion in those dark, brooding eyes—eyes Denise could happily have drowned in. And his mouth curved into a strange and secret smile that seemed to reach to the centre of her soul. 'But of course you know,' he murmured huskily, breaking the silence but quickening the spell. 'I'm simply following the lead you gave and setting the tone for the next two weeks. I'm going to show you,' he explained, lips brushing hers, touching, tasting, teasing, tantalising, 'how Adam Walker's fiancée is expected to behave when the rest of the world is looking on. And, Denise,' he added solemnly, 'I do believe that I'm going to enjoy each and every moment.'

CHAPTER TWO

'NO, ADAM,' she protested feebly as he pulled her into his arms.

His answer was a laugh, a low, husky laugh that rippled through his body, and as Denise tried to pull away he growled deep in his throat, arms closing round her, his mouth tracing searingly light kisses across her heated brow, across her brow and down the bridge of her nose, before hovering provocatively at the corner of her mouth.

'Oh, but yes, Denise,' he insisted, his breath a warm flutter on over-sensitive skin. 'Oh, but yes!'

She squirmed in his arms, rigid arms that held her fast as his mouth began to coax a reaction, made the merest hint of a connection as his lips met hers, a fleeting touch that was almost sheer imagination. Only Denise knew better, her traitorous body knew better, the heat flowing out from tiny points of contact, the thrill running through her like a tongue of molten steel. It was wrong, very wrong—Adam's lips so deliciously persuading, the touch, the taste so unbelievably good that Denise dredged deep for the strength to resist, the strength to deny, to repel.

'Don't,' he commanded huskily, indulgence threading the tone. 'Don't fight me, Denise. Don't fight what nature intended. Relax,' he urged, a languid tongue tracing the outline of her mouth. 'It's just a kiss—my lips touching yours, my tongue tasting yours, my mouth teaching yours to come alive. And you will come alive, I promise you, Denise, because the more you struggle, the more you'll lose—the more I'll fight to break your resistance. Just relax,' he crooned again as the pressure increased, insidiously, inevitably, the mesmeric words soothing and stirring, soothing and inciting. 'Relax, honey, relax.'

He stroked her cheeks, magic hands no longer restraining simply holding, caressing, a single thumb tracing the angle of her jaw, an unexpectedly tender touch that tugged at her heartstrings, and Denise moaned aloud as he cradled her face, the ebony eyes locking with hers, smouldering with emotion.

And then he kissed her, her lips parting with the shock and Adam's tongue sliding swiftly through. He tugged her roughly to him and she moaned again, her breasts pressed shamelessly against the powerful chest, shirt and blouse non-existent barriers as the currents surged and flowed, Adam's growl of pleasure music to her ears, his tongue finding hers, tasting hers, sweeping on into moist, inviting corners, a fervid exploration that promised so much more.

'Adam, Adam, Adam,' she mewed, common sense and sanity light-years away.

And he laughed—a deep, sensual chuckle that seemed to echo in her mind. 'Oh, Denise,' he murmured throatily. 'I knew you'd come alive. You had to be alive, somewhere deep inside. You look so good, taste so good, feel so good that you had to be made for loving, and I was right, my little temptress, wasn't I?' And the hungry lips moved on, nibbling, biting, caressing, branding where they touched, inciting where they touched, and as Denise moved her head from side to side a million tiny kisses feathered the stem of her neck, the pleasure exquisite, exciting and ensnaring.

And still there was more—exploring hands that slid from her shoulders, gliding across her curves, an ethereal touch that kindled new explosions, the passion flaring afresh. Adam's growl of satisfaction stirred the blood in her veins as his mouth found hers again, his magic fingers making music on her body, the urge to touch, to taste, to kiss, to love an overwhelming need that screamed out for satisfaction. Yet still he denied her, hands skirting the contours of her breasts, *almost* touching, *almost* caressing, *almost*. . . Her emotions were spiralling out of control as Adam stoked the flames. She wanted him! She needed him! And the rest of the world ceased to exist as body and soul combined. One mind, one thought, one need—Adam. And then the music faded, black eyes openly mocking as Adam pulled away.

She sobered at once. 'You rat!' she derided, the rawness of the pain catching her off-guard. 'You rat. You despicable rat.' And she rubbed her mouth with the back of her hand in an effort to wipe away the stain.

'You weren't exactly reluctant, Denise,' he pointed out calmly.

'No.' She angled her head, grey eyes flinty. 'And I don't suppose you're exactly short of practice—especially as you *are* engaged—or has that inconvenient fact slipped your mind?'

'How kind of you to remind me,' he drawled. 'And no, I hadn't forgotten that for the next few days at least I'm happily engaged to you.'

'Only for appearance's sake,' she pointed out swiftly. 'Anything else is a sham, a charade, and doesn't give you the right to do as you please.' She swallowed, the memory of the touch, the taste, the kiss—the need—echoing in her mind, the waves of guilt that followed providing the strength to harden her heart. 'Are you listening, Adam?' the chill voice demanded. 'An act for public is one thing,' she allowed. 'But touch me again, kiss me again when we're alone, and I'll walk out on you so fast you won't see my heels for dust. I'm not Jen,' she reminded him bitterly. 'And don't you *ever* dare forget it.'

He shrugged, his expression tight, unreadable, and he turned away, starting the car in silence.

They emerged from the underground car park into a pool of golden light and Denise blinked hard, the sunshine blinding, the residue of tears taking her by surprise. Fool, she inwardly railed. Allowing Adam near. He was simply playing games, having fun at her expense, and the anger surged afresh, bitter reproach of her own wild response whipping up the fury. Selfish, self-centred, totally absorbed, Adam Walker deserved everything he got. In fact, she decided harshly, he'd only himself to blame for the entire sorry mess. That Jen had been uncaring she now conveniently forgot. Let him hurt, let him sting, let him cope. Adam could join the ranks of the human race and learn how it felt to suffer. Pain? He didn't know the meaning of the word. And then she remembered. Adam was angry—worse than angry—and who could blame him? Jen had left him in the lurch, not caring that she'd hurt not only Adam but a vulnerable old lady as well. Hardly surprising that he'd turned, channelling his anger at the person left behind—Denise. Unfair of him, she knew, but he *would* calm down in time. And, if understanding led to forgiveness, Adam had already been absolved. Or at least, she amended painfully, the fire of Adam's touch and the magic of his kisses engraved on her mind, she would try.

They cruised to a halt a few moments later, her grey eyes widening as she registered the name of the exclusive Mayfair restaurant.

'It's past two,' Adam explained, sensing her surprise. 'And I'm hungry. We'll have lunch. Unless you're one of those faddy females who never touches food in the middle of the day?'

'With a figure like mine?' Denise scorned. 'Don't be ridiculous. Besides, think of your investment. All those highly expensive clothes would surely go to waste if your surrogate fiancée suddenly lost weight. And talking of clothes,' she pointed out sweetly,

'I'm a little under-dressed for a place like this—
don't tell me you hadn't noticed?'

'Hmm.' Black eyes narrowed as they travelled the
length of her, lazily, suggestively, over the checked
blouse with its film of clay dust, down one faded
denim leg and back up the other, his leisurely
perusal of her body a tangible caress that kindled
emotions she preferred to ignore. 'Maybe,' he
allowed with a ghost of a smile. 'And since the jeans
rule out my other lunchtime haunts, that leaves us
with a problem.'

'Not at all,' she demurred, with an impish toss of
the head. 'Follow me, Adam. You're not the only
one who's hungry, and I know just the place to go
for a first-class meal.'

'A burger bar!' he groaned wryly as Denise
marched briskly round the corner, up the steps and
into the familiar cheerful environment. 'Good grief,
woman, I haven't been inside one of these since I
was ten years old.'

'Then it's high time you learned what you've been
missing,' she chaffed. 'And that wallet can go back
where you found it,' she snapped. 'This one's on
me.'

'Cheers!' He raised a flimsy container of Coke and
Denise swallowed a smile, angling hers in equally
solemn toast before turning back to the food. She
wasn't just hungry, she was famished, remembering
that breakfast had been hours ago and nothing more
than the single slice of toast she'd grabbed while she

was working. Work. Her lips tightened. She'd had an order to complete—a delicate figurine she'd carefully packed and parcelled ready for sending on its way. The motorbike courier had passed Adam on the drive. Ten minutes either way and she'd have lost the commission as arrogant Adam Walker imposed his powerful presence, demanding attention, commanding attention and ruining her precious concentration—not to mention her means to make a living. Denise scowled.

'Something wrong?' Adam enquired, polishing off a burger and reaching for a second. 'Isn't the food to madam's taste? And to think you chose the venue,' he mocked. 'Another contrary-minded female who wouldn't know what she wanted if it hit her in the face.' He grinned, clearly goading, expecting Denise to rise, and, second-guessing his intentions, Denise forced a smile.

'Such chauvinistic views, Adam. Sorry to disappoint you, but I know exactly what I want from life, and if you and Jen could get along without me, I could do something about it.'

'Give me two weeks,' he pointed out evenly, 'and I'll never bother you again.'

Famous last words, she almost retorted, but at the sudden jolt of pain left the taunt unsaid. Two short weeks. Yet two weeks of Adam's unnerving company was more than she could stand. And then she remembered. It wasn't going to happen—not if Denise could help it.

They finished their meal in comfortable silence,

the next surprise occurring when Adam cleared the table.

'Fair's fair,' he pointed out, catching her reaction. 'You bought the food, I take care of the debris. Or doesn't Jenny pull her weight that way?'

'Fishing, Adam?' Denise drawled slyly. 'If you really want to know, Jen's careful to a fault. I cook; she eats. I wash the dishes; Jen sits back and lets me. What could be fairer than that?' she enquired as he threw back his head and laughed, the happy sound bouncing round the room, drawing smiles from the afternoon diners.

'Doesn't it bother you?' he asked, black eyes surprisingly solemn. 'Playing the poor relation, I mean. You didn't have to stay with Jen, did you, Denise, not once you'd finished at university? Why go back? Why let Jen impose? Why leave yourself open to exploitation?'

'I simply went home,' she pointed out stiffly. 'And when it comes to exploitation, Adam, I'm looking at an expert. Or doesn't it count when the boot's on the other foot?'

His face darkened, the shutters coming down over strangely probing eyes. 'Point taken,' he acknowledged tersely. 'And you're right—this time. But, believe me, it would never have happened but for Kate's fragile health. And I owe her such a lot, the least I could do is try to make her happy.'

'Oh?' Denise enquired warily.

'Little Orphan Adam,' he explained, the pain in his voice cutting her in two. 'You're not the only child left without parents. And Kate took me in, did everything she could to make my childhood happy. You had Jen,' he stated coldly, bleakly, accusingly. 'Not to mention Jen's money. You try growing up in two damp rooms with just the clothes on your back and stale bread in the larder before you lecture me on the finer points of exploitation. I am what life—and Kate—has made me,' he told her grimly. 'And I refuse to apologise for anything I've done, or will ever do for Kate.'

'Oh!' Colour flooded her face and she dropped her gaze, unable to parry the accusation in the pair of black eyes. She hadn't known. Jen had never said. Had Jen ever known? she wondered fleetingly. But of course she had. Only Jen, being Jen, would quickly block out the image of the vulnerable boy growing up in poverty. That life could be hard, Denise knew to her cost, but Jenny—beautiful, pampered Jen—had no idea of the sort of existence life meted out to so many children.

Denise swallowed hard. 'I'm sorry, Adam,' she murmured softly, raising her eyes and registering the pain etched across his features. He ignored her, staring rigidly out at the people passing by. His hand lay on the table, fist clenched hard, the knuckles showing white, and Denise reached out slowly, hesitantly, not sure she was doing the right thing and, almost on the point of drawing back, allowed a single, tentative finger to brush the taut skin. Adam turned his head, his eyes seeking hers, surprise giving way to something else, an unfathomable emotion that tugged at her heartstrings.

'I was wrong,' he admitted wryly, fingers relaxing as he captured her hand. 'You're nothing like Jen. You've proved it today time and again. But Kate doesn't know it and that's what counts. I need your help,' he stated simply, the eyes holding hers full of mute appeal. 'If you could bring yourself to give it?'

'I didn't think I had much choice,' she stalled, aware of the touch of skin on skin and the thrill that rippled through her as she met his solemn gaze.

'You haven't,' he agreed softly. 'Not if you're half the woman I think you are.' And when Denise raised a puzzled eyebrow he added with a smile, 'Your social conscience, remember? Unlike my thorny presence, Denise, it's something you'll be stuck with all your life.' He scraped back his chair, the tender moment over. 'Come on, let's make a move. The afternoon's half gone and we've a lot to get through. Kate might be old but there's nothing wrong with her eyesight, and the magic wand is poised for its next assignment.'

Leastways, that was what Adam was assuming. But Denise, social conscience or no, was about to dig in her heels.

'But you promised,' he pointed out slyly as they halted outside the salon.

'I promised to help,' she amended swiftly, surprised to find that she really did mean it. Until Jen came home she *would* help out, and if it reassured Adam to have Denise around, it wouldn't hurt to go along with him. 'But not like this. It won't work. I'm not a lump of clay to be teased and squeezed into a parody of my cousin. Can't you *see*?' she demanded. 'It won't work. I won't look right, won't feel right, won't act right. Why can't I be myself, for goodness' sake?'

'You can,' he insisted tersely. 'As long as you look the part. And a shampoo and set is hardly the end of the world.'

'Hah!' Grey eyes oozed derision. 'And the rest. I know you. You'll whip me inside and before I can blink my over-long, over-staid, over-mousy hair will have been cut, dried and bleached into oblivion. *You* might not approve,' she bit, with a defiant toss of the head, 'but it suits me and that's how I'd like to keep it.'

He shrugged. 'Fine. If that's what you want. But at least come inside and have a word with Tony. And if a shampoo and set is the most he can talk you into, well——' he shrugged again '—I guess I'll learn to live with it.'

'And you promise not to bully?'

He smothered a sigh, reaching out, fingers fastening on her shoulders, and the familiar rivulets of heat coursed through her veins. 'You don't trust me at all, do you, Denise?' he enquired flatly.

'Only as far as I can throw you, Adam,' she told him stiffly. 'If that.' And she shook herself free of the disconcerting touch, marching stiff-backed to the door.

Adam followed. 'Denise Elliot, Tony,' he introduced coolly. 'She's all yours. And be warned, she's one hell of a stubborn lady.' He nodded at Denise, his expression unbending. 'I'll pick you up at four,' the terse voice informed her. 'If I thought for a moment you'd listen to sense, I'd stay and offer my opinion. But go ahead. Dig in your heels. Tell the most talented stylist in London that he hasn't to touch a hair of your head, and walk out of here with all the aplomb of a wallowing hippopotamus. If you're happy, why should I care?'

Left alone, Denise caught the interest on a dozen staring faces—beautiful, pampered women, expensively groomed—and she bristled. A wallowing hippopotamus, hey? She'd show him. Jen or no Jen, Denise was going to that party and, in that case, she'd do it in style. Oh, Adam, she mocked inwardly as the assistant rinsed her hair. You could rue the day you tangled with this much too stubborn lady.

Only Adam, she quickly discovered, took the new and improved version all in his stride.

'Very nice,' he approved, with just a fleeting glance at the expensive transformation. Denise stiffened. Such faint and damning praise, she scorned. And then it hit her. Adam was much too adept at getting what he wanted—if not one way then another—and she sat grim-faced and silent as he edged the car into the early evening traffic. It was galling to admit, but there was more to Adam Walker than first met the eye. After all, hadn't Denise done exactly what he wanted?

* * *

'Jen! Thank heavens. I thought you'd never answer the phone. Where on earth have you been till now?'

'Working, remember? And now I'm feeling tired. If you don't mind, Denise, I need to lie down before dinner.'

'Oh, I'm sorry, Jen. I didn't think. I'd have left it till morning but since it concerns the engagement——'

'Engagement? What engagement?' Jen enquired harshly. 'It's off. Don't tell me you hadn't heard?' she added flippantly.

'But—it can't be,' Denise spluttered stupidly. 'Everything's arranged and Adam——'

'Can go to hell. I don't need him any longer, and if Adam's put you up to phoning, he's wasting his time. Everything I need is here.'

'But you love Adam,' Denise pointed out.

'Don't be ridiculous. Love never entered into it. It was—just convenient for both of us.'

'But——' Denise was growing desperate. Adam, Kate, two hundred guests all set to toast the happy couple. And surely Jen was wrong. An engagement was a promise, a pledge—not a cold and clinical arrangement. Yet it had come as a surprise, she remembered, her mind slipping back to her cousin's look of triumph just two short weeks before. Like the cat with the cream, Denise recalled, her heart sinking at the thought. What Jen wanted, Jen fought tooth and nail for, and then the novelty would fade and the toy would be tossed aside with never a moment's thought. Only this time Denise didn't want to believe it. 'Oh, Jen,' she pleaded softly. 'Adam needs you.'

'Oh, sure,' her cousin scorned. 'He's an arrogant man and he likes a pretty woman at his side—until the next one comes along. But Adam can think again. I've had enough. I quit.'

'You mean—you're not coming home?' Denise asked incredulously.

'To be bullied? Insulted? Oh, no! Adam and I are through. He made that perfectly clear in yesterday's phone call. Well, fine, I don't need need him any longer—not with Zak taking care of me.'

'Zak?' Denise queried, suddenly growing cold.

'Zak Peters. Fashion photographer. One of the best. I'm good for him; he's good for me. Together we can't go wrong. So you see, Denise. . .'

Denise did, only too clearly. Arrogant Adam had issued an ultimatum and Jen had defied him. No wonder he'd been furious. And as for Kate, poor Kate was getting caught in the cross-fire. And thinking of Kate, Denise made one last effort.

'Listen, Jen,' she began confidentially, 'couldn't you make your peace with Adam, just for a week or two? Kate flies in tomorrow and——'

'No, Denise!' Jen interrupted harshly. '*You* listen. I've had enough. You—Adam—Kate. I've a life of my own, in case you've forgotten, and if Adam needs a nursemaid to keep his grandmother happy, fine. *You* do the job. I'm staying put. And don't bother phoning again,' she instructed crisply, 'you'll be wasting your time.'

The phone went dead. Denise froze. Now she'd blown it. It had been a slim enough chance to start with, but wild horses wouldn't drag Jen home now. 'Idiot,' she berated herself. And then the careless words hit home. *Jen* had a life of her own? Who the *hell* did she think she was—issuing orders left, right and centre, arranging other people's lives without so much as a second thought? And she jumped up, pacing up and down with the pent-up fury of a tiger in a cage. For two pins she'd walk out now, leave Adam and Jen to their own selfish ways. She had work to do, too, she railed. Oh, nothing as high-profile as international modelling, but the business she'd created was important—to herself at least. And why not? Hadn't she worked hard, scrimping and scraping her way through university, saving every penny for the studio? And she'd done it, with a bit of help from Jen. Jen. The anger faded.

Self-centred, thoughtless Jen, who was generous to a fault. It had been Jen's idea to build the studio in the garden. Why waste money on rent? she'd insisted. And those early commissions had come from Jen's friends. Denise smothered a sigh. Elliot Ceramics might just pay its way, but she couldn't turn her back on Jen. With Adam poised to strike the moment Denise stepped out of line, Jen's career—with or without Zak Peters—was hanging by a thread.

Round one to Adam, she acknowledged grimly. But he'd better make the most of it, for Denise was learning fast.

* * *

'You look—almost presentable.'

Denise flushed. Adam was teasing, but as he led the way across the crowded restaurant the easy words began to bite. Heads turned, eyes following— female eyes that barely logged her existence before fastening hungrily on Adam—and alone in the crowd Denise felt the hurt grow. She didn't belong, she realised bitterly, amazed to discover that she really did mind.

Pride came to the rescue. It might be a sham, but just for now the most striking man in the room belonged to her, and, reaching their table she paused, aware of a silent expectation hanging in the air.

'Thank you, darling,' she retorted huskily and, smiling brightly up into that much too handsome face, offered her mouth for the kiss Adam wasn't expecting. It's your move, she silently goaded, grey eyes loaded with challenge. But Adam merely smiled, his confidence galling as he bent to brush her lips—or so he assumed until Denise snaked a hand around his neck. Faced with the choice of giving in or being made to look a fool, he allowed the kiss to deepen.

'Madam, I could wring your pretty neck,' he growled, catching her flash of triumph.

'But you won't, hey, Adam?' she needled. 'Because I'm simply following orders. And, since you're a man who likes value for money, why refuse the bonus?'

'Some bonus,' he murmured drily, but the hard

edge had left his tone, and Denise caught grudging admiration in the warm black eyes.

It set the tone for the meal, and Denise began to relax as an excellent claret coursed warmly through her veins. Jen's harsh words lost some of their sting and by the time they reached the cheese the thought of helping Adam didn't seem such a chore. Two short weeks, she reasoned, vaguely aware of the soft spot Adam held in her heart. Heaven alone knew why, given the lashings of arrogance, unless the man beyond the image occasionally pierced the shell. And, though still not convinced that she could carry the part, for Jen—and for Kate—Denise would try.

'Coffee?' Adam enquired as Denise popped the last creamy crumb of Stilton into her mouth.

She nodded. 'Mmm. Coffee would be lovely, and thank you, I enjoyed that.'

'So I gathered.' He smiled wryly. 'It also accounts for the fortune spent at Claud's. You don't do things by halves, do you, Denise?'

'Do you?' she countered coolly, the temperature dipping. 'And, just for the record, *I* didn't ask for charity. I'm doing you a favour just being here, Adam, and it wouldn't be wise to forget it.'

'Are you threatening me?'

'Not threatening, reminding. I've a business standing idle while I pander to your ego. And if a few outrageous clothes I didn't want, didn't need and will never wear again aren't worth the price, just say the word and I'll be off.'

'Why?' he enquired, perfectly calmly.

'Why what?' she snapped, annoyed at his composure and the vague idea that Adam was amused.

'Why consign them to the dustbin? They're beautifully cut, beautifully styled, and that dress, for one, is dateless. Think of the waste,' he chided lightly. 'You could wear it time and again in the next ten years and it wouldn't look out of place.'

'No, I don't suppose it would,' she agreed bitterly, reaching for the water-jug and filling her glass. 'But if the best that money can buy is wasted on me, why bother? "Almost presentable" I may be,' she reminded him, 'but in future, Adam, I'll do it my way.'

'Oh, I *see*.' Velvet eyes panned from stormy face to fluttering breasts and back again. 'The lady has pride—not to mention the teeniest bit of vanity. And why not, since tonight she's out of this world? It's a fact, Denise,' he nodded solemnly. 'And, what's more, you did it your way.'

'Oh, yes?' She blinked back the tears, too raw to take the words at face value. 'Don't lie, Adam. You don't have to pretend. Honesty's all we've got between us. Don't sacrifice that in the interests of peace. You paid for the dress, paid for the hair-style——'

'And left you to choose both, remember? And though you'd never pass for Jen——'

'No! I'm too plump, too staid, too mousy——'

'You're twisting what I said, Denise. And a size twelve is hardly overweight.'

'Wrong!' she contradicted harshly. 'I haven't been

that in years. I'm flattered. Unless,' she added bitterly, 'the comment's just a ploy?'

'To smooth ruffled feathers?' He shook his head. 'Oh, Denise, don't sell yourself short. I saw the heads turn as I followed you across the floor——'

'And so did I. And believe me, Adam, those Sindy-doll clones didn't waste a glance on me.'

'No.' He swallowed a smile. 'But the Sindy-doll companions did. And, before you toss out another denial, remember the camera never lies.'

He waved a lazy hand to the display of plants behind. A security camera, she realised quickly, spotting three or four more dotted about the room, cleverly concealed among the greenery, and she swallowed hard as her troubled gaze moved back to Adam's solemn face.

'If you won't believe me,' he chided softly, 'judge for yourself. I'll have one of the staff drop the tape in later. Watch it, Denise,' he commanded gently. 'You never know, you might just learn the truth.'

He's simply being kind, she told herself, dropping her eyes and focusing instead on the starched white cloth beneath the smattering of crumbs. Kind, tactful, manipulative. He was clever enough to flatter without going too far. She'd never be a beauty, would never follow Jen down a catwalk, would never stop a room dead as she walked through the door. She knew it and Adam knew it. But he couldn't afford to cross her. The fine clothes had procured respect, but they'd done nothing to disguise the ugly duckling. She shouldn't have agreed to help, she realised belatedly, swallowing the lump that threatened to choke her. But the longer the charade went on, the harder it would be to escape.

She smothered a yawn as they reached the marbled foyer. It had been a long day and the strain was beginning to tell.

'You're tired!' Adam accused. 'Silly girl, you should have said. Come on, time for bed.'

Bed! Denise bristled. Who did he think he was, ordering her upstairs like a four-year-old? And she opened her mouth to protest as Adam caught her hand.

'No arguments,' he insisted firmly. 'You're worn out—deny it if you dare.'

But she didn't get the chance, a husky voice sailing across and freezing the words in her mind. 'Adam! Jen!' the woman called delightedly, stepping nimbly across their path. And then she realised her mistake, the dazzling smile fading as her startled gaze switched from Adam's inscrutable face to Denise's hot and guilty one. Curious green eyes swept down, and though Denise did her best to free her hand Adam's grip tightened. It was a tense, nerve-racking moment. And then the woman smiled again, a muted smile of triumph. 'Oh, Adam,' she purred delightedly. 'Hold the front page. The Press is about to have a field-day.'

CHAPTER THREE

'DON'T say a word,' he ordered tersely as he guided her swiftly, efficiently, out of the woman's venomous presence. Denise risked a glance at the uncompromising profile, her heart lurching down to the floor. Adam wasn't angry, he was furious, and though Denise shouldn't feel responsible she was sickly aware that she did. She was Jen's cousin and she'd known what Jen was up to. Yet what could she have done? she silently entreated. Tied her down? Locked her in her room? In this day and age? Denise almost snorted. No, the idea was ridiculous. Jen was to blame—going off in search of fame and fortune, uncaring of the chaos left behind.

'It isn't going to work,' she pointed out bleakly as they reached the door to her room.

'Isn't it?' He smiled frigidly, slotting the coded key into the panel and following her inside. 'Stop looking for problems. The woman's a gossip, just a cheap and nasty hack.' He shrugged. 'She's not important.'

'Come off it, Adam. Sadie Graham's a friend of Jen's and you saw her face. She can't wait to blast some seedy story right across the tabloids.'

'And what if she does? It's hardly the end of the world.'

46

No, she didn't suppose it was—for Fleet Street's newest proprietor. Gossip meant news, news sold papers, papers meant money—for Adam.

'Maybe not,' she agreed bitterly. 'But the woman's poison. She'd sell her soul to the highest bidder and she'll twist what she's seen into something sordid. You might not care but I do. Besides, think of Kate.'

'I've told you, quit worrying.' He shrugged again. 'Kate can't abide the British Press. If World War Three were announced next week, Kate wouldn't be any the wiser. In any case, what could that sleazy woman imply? That Adam Walker was wining and dining his bride-to-be?'

'Ah, yes! But which one, Adam? Or is it a case of off with the old and on with the new? Makes quite a headline, don't you think?' she added sweetly. 'Of course, if I'd known you and Jen were through——'

'You'd have turned me down flat, I suppose,' he interrupted drily. 'Don't flatter yourself, Denise. The job's not for real. It's a two-week contract and you didn't have a choice. Not if you care about Jen—or Jen's money,' he tossed out slyly.

'Meaning?' Denise went cold.

'Come now, don't be coy. This is Adam you're dealing with. You can't fool me. Denise Elliot, the independent little cousin, who goes her own way and copes all alone yet quietly takes whatever Jen will give. The university course, the studio, the business. Each and every penny paid by Jen—hey, Denise?'

She shrugged. 'Maybe you're right,' she admitted stonily, grey eyes full of silent scorn.

The generous mouth curved into another mocking smile. 'I *know* I'm right. And the fact that you're here speaks for itself. Elliot Ceramics,' he declared sneeringly, 'stands on the brink. If Jen falls, you fall, and the cushioned existence comes to an end—for both of you.'

'Really?' Her voice was cool, though she couldn't shake the notion that Adam could be right. Only he was bluffing. If he cared about Jen, he *had* to be bluffing, and yet Denise wasn't sure. Where Adam was concerned she wasn't sure of anything, not any more.

'Yes, really. I know it and you know it, and in that case, Denise, you'll do as you're told. Choice is a luxury you just can't afford—not with Jen.'

'Ah, yes, Jen. The ghost at the feast—or should it be the engagement party?' she drawled with quiet irony.

'Irrelevant. You'll be there, and that's all that matters.'

'Will I?'

'Oh, yes. There's too much at stake for you to walk away. You're an Elliot, and smugly convinced that life owes you a living—the easy way. And since Jen holds the purse-strings, well. . .' He shrugged, the careless confidence galling, yet another provocation she had to ignore. Because Adam, clever, clever Adam, was goading her again.

'So Jen has a hold over me,' she allowed. 'Why

not? I owe her a lot and we were brought up like sisters. You, of course,' she slipped in much too sweetly, 'have a different excuse.'

'And what's that supposed to mean?'

'Exactly what it says.' She raised her shoulders in her own eloquent goad. 'I've heard love is blind, Adam, but it couldn't really addle the brain of a self-made millionaire—or could it?' she softly challenged.

His face changed, the shutters dropping down at once. 'Mind your own business,' he all but snarled and, subject closed, he swung away. Off came the jacket, followed by the tie, and Denise watched warily as long, slender fingers loosened the collar of the crisp white shirt, the casual result strangely electric, a careless intimacy that Denise found disturbing.

Make yourself at home, she inwardly derided, needing a diversion for wayward thoughts. Since Adam was paying the bill, Adam would call the tune, and Denise would grin and bear it. Maybe, she amended tersely, logging the opulence, the wall to wall luxury. The room was heaven on earth—soft white leather sofas and smoked-glass tables on a sea of ivory wool. Maybe. And just maybe he would push her too far.

'I need a drink,' Adam stated baldly, heading for the mini-bar. He picked out the brandy. 'May I?'

Denise nodded. 'Of course,' she granted coolly. 'But make mine a vodka. A dash of tonic, a slice of lemon and lots and lots of ice.' She didn't wait for a reaction, turning away and crossing to the windows where she pushed aside the blinds. The lights of the city were spread out beneath, familiar landmarks etched against a star-studded canvas.

'I didn't think you drank vodka,' he queried frostily, handing her a glass.

'Well, there you are.' Grey eyes flashed derision. 'You're learning something new. And surprise, surprise, Adam Walker doesn't know the real me after all. How galling.'

'Not at all. As I've told you already, I know more than you'd imagine. And if a gap does exist, I'll worm the knowledge out of you—one way or another.'

'Oh, yes?' Denise smiled grimly. That was what *he* thought.

'Oh, but yes!'

Impasse. Two people. Two minds—yet the same iron will to retain the upper hand. And Adam was supremely sure that he was in control. Like all rich men, he measured success in money, blithely assumed that everyone had their price. But he was wrong. Only Adam, self-assured, arrogant Adam, would never be convinced. And the stark fact was that it didn't matter. Adam refused to believe and Denise didn't care. She knew. She had her life, she had her work, she had Jen, and she'd happily live in a garret as long as she had the means to pay the rent and keep herself from starving. And if she did go through with this ridiculous charade, it wasn't for a reason Adam would understand.

He drained his glass. 'I'd better be going. I've a busy day ahead—*we've* a busy day ahead. Assuming you haven't changed your mind?'

'Worried, Adam?' she couldn't resist needling. 'You really don't know, do you?' she scoffed. 'You're almost sure I'm cornered, but at the back of your mind there's a shadow of doubt. Because what Adam Walker wants, Adam Walker buys. Only this time,' she pointed out slyly, 'the lady's not for sale. This time, it's all down to conscience. *My* conscience, *my* debt to Jen—and a moral obligation to a woman I've yet to meet. I wonder what odds they'd quote for a risk as wide as the ocean?'

'You're wrong,' he coolly retorted. 'Jen's the risk. You're the certainty.'

Am I? she silently scorned, and then something crossed her mind. 'Tell me,' she invited cosily, 'what happens later? When the wedding of the year has been pencilled on to the calendar? If Kate can't handle a broken engagement, how will she take the news that her grandson's ditched the bride?'

His face changed, the shadow of pain so swiftly replaced by anger that Denise couldn't be sure she'd seen it.

'Kate's ill, very ill,' he stated bluntly. 'And she won't be around for a wedding. Didn't Jen bother to explain?' he demanded. 'But no,' he muttered grimly, before Denise had time to speak, 'she'd rather not face the harsher side of life, so what she doesn't like, she ignores.'

'Oh, Adam!' Denise was horrified. 'I didn't know, didn't realise——'

'No,' he interrupted harshly. 'You wouldn't. Like Jen, you're too wrapped up in your own cosy self.'

'That's not fair,' she found herself protesting.

'Fair?' He was on his feet in an instant, towering above her, his whole expression ugly. '*Fair*? Jen turns her back on a frail old woman and you talk to me about fair? Grow up, Denise. This is life in the real world.' He laughed as she shrank into the cushions, a cold, harsh blast of derision that froze the blood in her veins. 'Welcome to the real world,' he murmured evilly, rigid fingers cupping her chin, a bruising, upward snatch that sent her head snapping back in alarm. 'And now that you're in it,' he chillingly informed her, black eyes raining hate, 'don't even try to walk away.' The iron grip tightened and Denise went white as Adam's ugly, snarling face was thrust against hers. 'Are you listening, damn you?' the vicious voice demanded. 'Let Kate down too, and you'll wish you'd never been born.'

He released her, contempt oozing from each and every pore, and as the door slammed to behind him Denise crumpled. Oh, Jen, she silently upbraided, brushing away the tears. What have you done? It wasn't true. It couldn't be. Selfish, thoughtless— yes! Jen had her faults, but to walk out on Adam at a time like this? No. Denise shook her head. Jen couldn't have known, she consoled herself. Not even her empty-headed cousin could turn her back on a dying woman. And yet, she acknowledged sickly, if Adam was telling the truth, that was how it seemed.

They drove north in silence, Adam's profile uncompromisingly grim. It was a tense ninety minutes, the cool, grey morning a perfect match for Adam's mood. As they pulled on to the drive of his impressive Shropshire home a ray of sunlight came out to greet them. An omen, perhaps? Denise mused wryly, following Adam inside. She was relieved to discover that he wasn't staying.

'Maria will look after you,' he explained quickly, treating the older woman to the sort of smile that made Denise go weak at the knees. 'If there's anything you need, just ask. I'll be back this afternoon—with Kate. My other house-guests won't arrive till six. In the meantime, make yourself at home.'

Left alone, there was nothing she could do but follow Maria's silent form across the hall and up the elegant marble staircase, reluctantly approving the opulent décor, the airy lines of the house. It was built on the banks of the Severn, a Victorian folly that Adam had transformed into a small country mansion, and, though clearly a show-piece, it somehow retained a warm and friendly feel.

'Oh, how beautiful,' Denise exclaimed when Maria led the way into a bedroom.

The housekeeper frowned, cool green eyes flicking from the canopied bed, fit for a queen, to the range of matching furniture. 'Yes,' she agreed curtly. 'It's the nicest room in the house, although the young miss never seemed to think so. Still, she's old enough to know her own mind,' she muttered sourly, and though the sniff of disapproval didn't follow Denise could almost hear it. Maria moved, marching stiff-backed to the door. 'I'll leave you to get on. Lunch will be served on the terrace. One o'clock sharp.'

Yes, ma'am! Denise resisted piping, and then she scowled. She clearly wasn't welcome, though if Maria's cryptic tone was any guide neither was Jen. And as for Adam. . . Denise stifled a sigh. One way or another, it wasn't going to make for the easiest of stays.

The rap on the door took her by surprise. 'I've come to help you unpack, miss,' the fresh-faced girl explained.

'Oh!' Denise flushed. There had been daily staff at her aunt and uncle's but, though Jen had taken them for granted, Denise had looked after herself. And with most of her clothes coming straight from the boutique, there was little enough for Denise to do. 'I think I can manage,' she insisted softly, rustling up a smile. 'But thanks all the same. . .?'

'Jilly,' the girl supplied, her manner a lot more welcoming than Maria's. 'Well, if you're sure. . .?'

Denise nodded. 'I'm sure.'

Despite the urge to spin it out, the task was soon over, and since it was nowhere near lunchtime Denise was left with nothing to do. She could always explore the house, she supposed, take Adam at his word and make herself at home, but she wasn't sure she had the right. She felt like an intruder, as if she didn't belong—which she didn't, she acknowledged grimly. But why let that worry her? And, following her nose, she made her way down to the kitchen.

'Help?' Maria murmured incredulously. 'But you're a guest. Besides, there's little enough for me to do. The place is full of agency staff, poking and prying and getting in the way. No, miss,' she insisted firmly. 'You just relax. Jilly and I can manage, thank you.'

Denise shrugged. 'I'll try,' she told her frankly. 'And I'm Denise. And if you do change your mind, I'd be more than happy to pull my weight.' She smiled, praying for a hint of a thaw in Maria's cool green eyes. It didn't happen, but something in the older woman's manner led her to believe that once respect was earned, it would be acknowledged.

Happier than she'd been all morning, Denise wandered out to the terrace. She'd read. She'd bought a book at the hotel shop, resisting the urge to flick through the morning papers, though judging from the headlines Sadie Graham's scoop hadn't made front-page news. With luck it never would, Denise had reassured herself, and then she'd shrugged. Who was she trying to kid? Sadie Graham was trouble—trouble with a capital T. She'd use her story all right—when she was good and ready—and only a fool would refuse to believe it. Still, if Adam wasn't bothered, why let it worry her? She opened her book, the latest P.D.James, and in a matter of minutes was miles away.

'So this is where you're hiding.' Adam's tone bore more than a hint of reproach. 'It didn't take long to adapt to the new role, did it, Denise?'

'Meaning?' She was instantly wary. She hadn't heard the car—who would with an engine that purred so softly? And, bracing herself to meet those mocking, scornful eyes, she returned his gaze, unblinking.

'Denise Elliot, lady of leisure. Like Jen, you could have been born to the part—hey, Denise?'

'If you say so,' she retorted crisply. 'And while dragging Jen into every other sentence is perfectly understandable, isn't it risky—assuming Kate's arrived?'

'Kate's lying down,' he informed her coolly. 'She did want to meet the blushing bride-to-be, but the trip wore her out and the besotted fiancé overruled her.' He smiled grimly, the black eyes holding hers full of silent scorn. 'So for now it's just you and me. Quite the cosy twosome.' And he flung himself down in a chair, pouring a glass of chilled lemonade from the jug Maria had left on the table.

Denise bit back an angry retort. Adam was angry. Not with her, she realised instinctively. Jen—the engagement—life's cruel twists. Adam had a right to be annoyed.

'Why not postpone the party?' she suggested softly. 'If Kate's not feeling up to it.'

'You don't know Kate. A party she's here for; a party she'll expect.'

'Fair enough,' Denise replied. 'But we don't have to rush things. Why not leave it a week or two, give Kate time to——?'

'No!' Adam's face was dark, and Denise felt herself rise.

'Why, Adam? Why? Why not listen to sense? It's the logical thing to do, and when——'

'Leave it, Denise,' he instructed curtly.

'Oh, certainly, sir,' she mockingly derided, adding a smart salute. 'Your word is my every command, my liege. But not until I've had my say. Jen——'

'Might change her mind?' he enquired dangerously. 'Might have a pang of conscience? It's too late,' he reminded her bitterly. 'Kate needs her now. Not next week, next month, next year. *Now*. Don't you see?'

'Oh, I see all right,' she conceded harshly. 'That arrogant nose has been pushed out of joint and this is your way of hitting back. No wonder Jen refused to listen. Two weeks, Adam, two short weeks—that's all she was asking. *Couldn't* you have postponed it?'

'Not for Jen, not for you, not for all the tea in China,' he scathingly replied. 'The answer, Denise, is no. End of subject.'

Denise let rip. 'You really are the most mulish, pig-headed, unyielding, obstinate, overweening man I've ever had the misfortune to meet, and for two pins, Adam, I'd pack my bags and leave you to it.'

'You missed out stubborn,' he pointed out mildly, aware that her anger had blown itself out.

'I was saving that for later,' she riposted. 'My parting-shot before I slam the door.'

'Only you won't, will you, Denise?'

'Won't I?' She raised her head, the tilt of her chin unwittingly aggressive.

Adam swallowed a smile. 'You honestly believe I'm just plain awkward, don't you?'

'And aren't you?'

There was a long, long pause, the expression in his eyes a curious mix of pain and hesitation, and Denise held her breath, aware of a battle taking place in his mind. There was something else, something she didn't understand but sensed, something important he'd chosen not to say. To Jen, too? she wondered, watching the shadows chase across his brow, and she sat perfectly still, waiting for Adam.

With a muttered oath he moved suddenly, the scrape of metal on concrete scything the air.

'Adam?' she probed as he reached the edge of the terrace, everything about him screaming dejection. He leaned against the wall, gazing down at the river, hardly moving, hardly breathing, and as the minutes ticked away and still he didn't speak Denise felt the unexpected sting of tears. Adam was hurting. She didn't know why and probably never would, she acknowledged grimly, but she'd never forget that glimpse of desolation in the depths of his eyes. And then he spoke.

'There was—someone I cared for,' he began

quietly, hesitantly, the need to explain costing him dear. 'Someone special. She was young, pretty, full of life and fun and, like sweethearts the world over, we made plans. Such wonderful plans,' he added in torment. 'Castles in the air. But we were young and we could dream, and I *would* make it happen. Somehow. Somehow I'd find the money to escape the smell of poverty. I did, too,' he added viciously, his clenched fist pounding the brickwork—punching, punishing, purging. 'But it was too late. I'd left it too late.'

'Don't,' Denise implored, feeling the pain and powerless to help. 'Please, Adam, you don't have to explain. Not to me, not now—not ever.'

He didn't seem to hear, the words going on, the voice low and anguished and tearing her apart. 'Celeste was ill, and, yes, by then I could afford the operation. But the money didn't help,' he conceded bitterly. 'She'd lived too long in the slums and she never stood a chance.'

Denise went cold. She knew. Heaven alone knew how, but she knew where Adam was leading, and she hugged her arms to her body in an effort to ward off the chill.

'She didn't come through,' he explained simply. 'I let her down.'

Denise moved, standing beside him, silently supporting, fighting the urge to reach out and touch. She wanted to cradle his head against her shoulder, hold, comfort, caress, smooth away the lines, take away the pain. Only she didn't have the right. But she was there, and she could listen, and she could share the moment.

'She never came through,' he said again. And then he turned to face her. '*Now* do you see?' he demanded harshly, the fingers on her shoulders forged out of steel. 'Next to Kate, she was the most important person in the world, and I swore then that I'd never let another woman close. I couldn't take the risk, couldn't take the pain. And now the gods are seeking their revenge.'

'Kate?' Denise queried as the penny dropped.

'She's here for exploratory neurosurgery,' he explained. 'At the Midland. She goes in next week. So you see. . .'

Denise did, but Adam was wrong, she was sure of it. 'It isn't going to happen,' she insisted urgently. 'Not to Kate. It was a tragedy, Adam, but it won't happen again. Please, Adam, you've got to believe it.'

'Have I?' His eyes were pools of torment, and as Denise gazed mutely, imploringly into their troubled depths the hands on her shoulders tightened their grip. The tension mounted, the atmosphere so thick she could have cut it with a knife, and then, unexpectedly, thankfully, Adam half smiled. 'I've tried, Denise. Believe me, I really have tried.'

She blinked hard as he released her, moving heavily back to the table.

'Lemonade?' he asked, tilting the jug, and Denise nodded. The moment had passed, but she'd never forget the pain, Adam's need to explain. She was touched. And yet, she realised starkly, who else could Adam confide in? Jen? Kate? Her lips twisted bitterly. No. He was alone with the shadows of the past, and in the dark hours of the night he'd be the loneliest man in the world. Poor Adam. And how ironic. How cruelly ironic. He'd worked hard to build up a fortune and he'd fight tooth and nail for Kate, but at the end of the day all the money in the world wouldn't help.

He filled her glass, their fingers touching as he passed it across, and as shivers of heat spread out from the point of contact Denise stifled a cry. This was ridiculous, she silently chaffed, gulping the ice-cold liquid. Sympathy, yes—they were both feeling raw—but she'd caught the scent of danger and was suddenly afraid.

'So, what do you think of the place?' Adam enquired, unaware of the tension quivering on the air.

'It's—superb,' she acknowledged frankly. Her voice wasn't quite steady but Adam wouldn't notice; he had too much on his mind to think about Denise and, if Adam could rustle up small-talk with his heavy heart, the least she could do was follow his lead. 'I hadn't realised that a river could be so busy yet so peaceful.'

'Did Maria show you round, or did you take yourself?' he asked, and Denise felt the blush rise.

'Neither,' she explained defensively. 'Maria was busy and I didn't like to pry. It seemed. . .well.

nosy, I suppose,' she ended feebly, aware from his expression that she'd said the wrong thing.

'More sensitive sensibilities,' he mocked. 'And equally misplaced. This is my home, Denise, and supposedly yours in the very near future. Didn't it cross your mind that Kate would want a guided tour with you? All weddings and girls' talk and getting-to-know-you conversation?'

'I——'

'Didn't think,' he interrupted wearily, and then he sighed, smothering the spurt of irritation. 'Come on. Let's do it now. And next time, Denise, try to remember why you're here.'

As if I could forget, she inwardly derided, following in silence.

It was another world, Jen's home paling in comparison. And if the house was enough to take her breath away then the gardens, the tennis courts, the private mooring on the river, not to mention the swimming-pool, were something else again. Yet a house that lay empty for most of the week seemed a waste. It felt—lonely, she decided absurdly. There was something missing—people, noise, bustle—something she couldn't put her finger on. And then they reached the library, a beautifully panelled room lined with books.

'Oh, Adam,' she breathed in wonder. 'How wonderful. Books, books, and still more books. You don't know how lucky you are.'

'Don't I?' he murmured indulgently as Denise

moved round, running her fingers along the leather-bound spines.

She reached for her favourite, *Pride and Prejudice*, subconsciously noting the well-thumbed pages. 'This is my idea of heaven,' she breathed. 'But I don't suppose Jen ever crossed the threshold.'

'No,' Adam agreed drily. 'If Jen had had her way, this room would have gone. She had plans for a fitness studio.'

'Oh, no!' Denise was horrified. 'But you couldn't—you wouldn't have. Would you?' she asked with new humility, and again, 'Would you, Adam?'

'What do you think?' he asked, coming near, taking the book, closing it and replacing it on the shelf. He folded his arms, a hint of a smile on generous lips. 'Come on,' he entreated playfully, 'don't be coy. Tell me what you really think. Is Adam Walker a Philistine—or what?'

She lowered her eyes, suddenly aware that he'd backed her into a corner, every instinct quiveringly alert, the fight-flight surge of adrenalin coursing through her veins. She wanted to bolt yet realised she was stranded. Move, and Adam would simply reach out a hand to stop her; hold her ground, and she was doomed. For Adam was playing games. Like a cat with a mouse he was teasing, testing, watching, but as the minutes ticked away and still nothing happened her nerve failed. She raised her eyes, slowly, oh, so slowly over the length of his long, jeans-clad legs, thigh muscles rippling beneath the faded denim. Higher and higher her gaze went, past the slender hips, across the powerful chest and the open-necked shirt, where a shadow of hair at the base of his throat beckoned irresistibly, the urge to reach out and touch so urgently compelling that she had to clamp clenched fists to her sides in an effort to stay in control. And, determined not to meet those far too knowing eyes, Denise stared rigidly ahead.

'Oh, Denise,' he murmured throatily, laughter threading the velvet. 'You can't disappoint me now, my little tigress. Tell me what you think; tell me what you feel. Come on, don't be shy. I think my ego can take it.'

'Only *think*? she goaded recklessly, grey eyes oozing scorn. 'What happened to the lashings of arrogance that Adam Walker wears like a crown? Or has Jen walking out knocked it all for six?'

Oh-oh, she realised belatedly as his mouth tightened, the expression in his eyes changing like the wind.

'You know,' he murmured confidentially, 'that tongue of yours is much too sharp, and one of these days you'll overstep the mark. And then. . .' He paused and smiled—a mocking, taunting, goading smile that she simply had to rise to.

'And then?'

He took a step nearer, slowly, deliberately, holding her gaze with his own. 'And then,' he murmured huskily, 'the caustic little cousin could well be taught a lesson—by me.'

'You don't say,' she drawled, sharp eyes gauging the distance to the door. And, deciding she had nothing to lose, tilted her chin in defiance. 'Oh, but, Adam,' she taunted softly, 'you'll have to catch me first—won't you?'

She sprang away before she'd finished speaking, excitement running in her veins and, convinced she'd escaped, laughter gurgled in her throat. Too soon! Just as she'd feared—hoped? she fleetingly wondered—a hand snaked out, clamping her wrist in a circle of iron, bringing her up sharp.

'Denise,' he murmured huskily, tugging once, tugging twice, before pausing deliberately, provokingly, and the third and final jerk bringing them face to face. 'Foolish, foolish words,' he drawled, hands sliding from wrist to elbow, holding, caressing, urging her closer and closer and closer. And as Denise licked her lips, the panic rising in her throat, Adam smiled. 'Foolish child,' he gently chided, dipping his head and tasting her mouth, his tongue tracing the quivering outline before strong arms closed round her, holding, trapping, and his mouth pressed down, the currents surging afresh between them. It was wonderful—the touch, the taste, the fire in her veins. It was bliss, sheer bliss.

And then she remembered. How could she? How could she flirt and tease, and worse, allow Adam to kiss her, *want* Adam to kiss her? And she froze, denying the voice inside that whispered that it couldn't be wrong, that hinted at a truth she wasn't ready to face.

'Oh, no, you don't,' Adam rasped, raising his head, black eyes pinning her. He caught her arms and shook her, none too gently. 'Oh, no, you don't,' he said again, cruel fingers biting deep. But the pain was forgotten as his mouth sought hers, harshly, hungrily, and as the lips relaxed their pressure, now coaxing and caressing, seeking a response and forcing a response as, with a tiny mew of protest, the last of her resistance drained away.

A low growl filled her ears; the strong arms were holding and enfolding now, no longer restraining, just cherishing as Adam touched, stroked, stoked the ripples of heat spiralling out from each and every point of contact, filling her with joy, an unbelievable emotion that screamed both right and wrong.

She raised her hands, cradling his neck, fingers raking the silken locks of hair, stroking, massaging, subconsciously urging his mouth to meld with hers, needing the taste, craving the bitter-sweet pain of Adam's touch, Adam's tongue exploring moist and secret depths.

'Oh, Denise,' he murmured thickly, drawing back, triggering another whimper of protest. Probing eyes searched her face, stripping away the layers, laying bare her soul. The moment was time-less, and as Denise gazed mutely, imploringly, into his eyes Adam dipped his head.

'You're unbelievable,' he told her solemnly. 'Denise, you're out of this world.' And then he smiled, a slow and sensual smile that tugged at her heartstrings, before reaching out again, touching, tasting, dropping searingly light kisses along the line of her jaw, every tiny point of contact exquisite torment, exquisite delight. Denise shivered at the touch, her body pressing into his, the needs of the flesh driving away the dictates of her mind.

'Adam! Adam! Adam!' she moaned, writhing against him, shockingly aware of the hands beneath her blouse, scalding, searing, blazing a trail upwards and outwards, nearer and nearer to Denise's straining breasts. And as he paused, fingers tantalisingly close to the centre of her existence, again she cried, 'Oh, Adam!'

'I want you,' he murmured hoarsely. 'It shouldn't have happened, but heaven help me, woman, I want you.' And he shook her roughly, eyes glowing like coals. 'Are you listening, damn you?' he demanded fiercely. 'Because I want you, Denise. And what Adam Walker wants, Adam Walker takes. Understand?'

CHAPTER FOUR

'CHILDREN!' the laughing voice chastised. 'This won't do at all. Why, anyone could be passing, and it's easy to guess what's running through your minds. In broad daylight, too! How divine!'

'Ah, Kate.' Adam smiled ruefully, releasing Denise at once and crossing the room to his grandmother. 'My apologies. I guess we've been caught in what the gossip sheets would quaintly term a compromising situation.'

'Don't even think it,' she demurred, eyes crinkling with indulgence as they rested on her grandson. 'The crime's all mine—poking my nose into other people's business. And at my age, Adam, I should know better.' She patted his cheek, part affection, part reassurance, allowing her gaze to slide past and find Denise, who'd used the time Kate had given her to pull herself together. 'And this, of course, must be Denise. My dear, you don't know how delighted I am to meet you.'

She swept forward before Denise had time to react and, gathering her into a surprisingly strong embrace, raised a cheek for the kiss Denise obligingly gave.

'Welcome to England, Mrs Walker,' Denise murmured awkwardly.

'Kate, my dear. The whole world calls me Kate. And I shall call you Denise. Adam can please himself what he calls you in private, but Denny's such a harsh name. In fact,' she told her confidentially, linking arms and drawing Denise back across the room, 'thanks to gremlins on the phone lines, I've spent the past three months convinced that your name was Jenny!'

A bemused Adam led them out to the terrace, though Denise was careful not to meet his eye. Round two to Adam, she inwardly acknowledged. He'd overcome the hurdle without so much as a word, and for the first time in what felt like days Denise began to relax. Maybe, just maybe, she grudgingly admitted, Adam's improbable scheme wasn't doomed to failure after all.

'So,' Kate demanded once tea had arrived, 'when's the happy day? You do have one in mind, I hope?'

'Well, not exactly——'

'Of course, we have——'

They spoke together, Denise blushing guiltily as Kate's shrewd brown eyes fastened on her face.

Kate leaned forward, patting her hand. 'Men!' she derided in an audible whisper. 'Will they never learn that when it comes to weddings and babies they should take a tip from children and be seen and not heard? So?' she persisted as Denise smothered a giggle.

Denise turned to Adam, but he was giving nothing away, his expression carefully neutral, so, mentally crossing her fingers, she took the plunge. 'We haven't made our minds up yet. A winter wedding, maybe, but something small and private. Adam may be used to crowds, but I find them overpowering, and with half the country invited tonight, well——' She shrugged, tossing him a look of pure defiance. 'If a girl can't organise her own wedding, what can she do?'

'Exactly!' Kate beamed approval. 'And I'm glad to hear you won't let Adam bully you.'

It was a pleasant half-hour, the sun warm on their backs, the conversation light and easy. Kate chatted happily—interesting tales about her travels. She had a flair for a story and a keen sense of humour, and Denise almost ached from the laughter. Until Kate mentioned plans for the future—a future she might never see.

It was a sobering thought. And yet, Denise realised, choking back the tears, Kate looked so healthy, the lines of her face radiating character, her natural animation belying the truth.

'Adam, she's wonderful,' she couldn't help but say once Kate had gone to change.

'Hmm,' he murmured sardonically. 'And I wouldn't mind betting that's what she thinks of you. Talk about mutual admiration. Heaven knows what I've let myself in for allowing you to meet. And what's this about a quiet winter wedding?'

'Ah!' Denise went pink. She shrugged. 'You kept me in the dark, Adam. For the man who thinks of everything, there are definite flaws in your reasoning. It was the obvious thing for Kate to ask. What else could I say?' she argued defensively. 'I know nothing about Kate except that she's ill, seriously ill, and needs to know that her grandson's settled. And since Jen wanted a Christmas wedding——' She broke off, aware from the set of his mouth that she'd said the wrong thing, and, stifling a sigh, poured herself another cup of tea.

'Really?' he enquired harshly. 'Well. I wonder who the lucky man is? Because it certainly won't be me.'

Denise didn't reply. Adam was stinging and the subject was taboo. Hurt pride? she wondered. Or something else, something more basic? Love, perhaps? she probed experimentally, the resultant stab of pain so unnerving that she quickly closed her mind. Then, when she judged that the anger had waned, she asked simply, 'How long has Kate got?'

'Four months, unless they operate, and even then there are no guarantees. So she's doing what she can while the pain's in control. And when it becomes too much——' He paused, the anguish on his face almost more than she could stand. 'She'll book into a clinic somewhere. Typical Kate,' he tagged on drily, 'hell-bent on doing things her way. I wanted to be with her but she turned me down flat. Work could go to hell, but Kate wouldn't allow it. Said it would be something to hold on to when she's gone, and she's right, I suppose. So you see. . .'

Denise did, the lump growing in her throat and

threatening to choke her. Life really wasn't fair, was it? she asked herself, and blinking away the salty trickle brought her gaze back to Adam. 'I'm beginning to understand,' she told him frankly. 'I thought you were playing games, overreacting, hitting back at Jen for walking out. But you're not. All you want is for Kate to go home happy.'

'She isn't going home,' he reminded her starkly, pushing back his chair and getting to his feet.

Alone, and never more lonely, Denise felt the sob rise. If she had to stand in a queue behind Adam, she'd wring Jenny's neck once she did arrive back, and she hoped for her cousin's sake that she didn't choose to show her face at just the wrong moment. With Sadie Graham's nose for a story, the idea of Jen back in England, with or without Zak Peters, didn't bear thinking about.

The phone call came through as Denise stepped out of a richly scented bath and, wrapping herself in the fluffy towelling robe that someone—Maria, she supposed—had thoughtfully provided, she reached for the hand-set at the side of her bed.

'Denise?' The unmistakable voice of her cousin came blasting down the line, and Denise visibly winced. Someone sure wasn't happy. 'What the *hell* do you think you're doing?' Jen demanded. 'I couldn't believe it when Sadie Graham rang——'

'Ah, yes. The dear lady herself. I wondered how long it would take for her to get in touch. And which particular words of poison has Sadie been spreading this time?'

'You know. Don't pretend you don't,' her cousin almost spat. And then the tone changed. 'Oh, Denise,' she wailed, with all the pathos of a wounded animal. 'How *could* you?'

'How could I what?' Denise enquired evenly. 'How could I hope to take the place of my glamorous cousin? How could I attempt to fool a sick old lady? Or how dare I spend the night in the same hotel as Adam? Don't worry,' she reassured her acidly, 'we had separate rooms.'

'*That* never worried me,' Jen told her bluntly. 'I've told you before, Adam has eyes for me and me alone, and if he did need a woman to keep his bed warm it certainly wouldn't be you.'

'Oh, I see,' Denise drawled coolly, more hurt than she cared to acknowledge, 'Adam can play the field as long as he's discreet, is that it? And as long as the woman doesn't hang around for an encore?'

'He's a virile man,' Jenny told her confidentially. 'And if I choose to ignore one or two indiscretions, that's up to me. Once we're married, naturally things will be different.'

'Oh, naturally,' Denise echoed, stunned, and then the anger surged. 'But don't forget, Jen,' she reminded her harshly, 'the engagement's off. Adam's free to do as he likes.' And then it struck her. 'Unless you've had a change of mind?' she asked, not sure that she wanted to know. 'You're flying home—is that why you're ringing?'

'Wrong!' her cousin informed her swiftly. 'I've a job to do, believe it or not. I know Adam was angry, but he'll come round when I'm voted model of the year. And I'll do it, Denise. This time.'

'Look, Jen,' Denise began, as reasonably as possible, 'I know your career's important but there's plenty of time. You're young, you're beautiful, you've the rest of your life in front of you. Kate hasn't,' she told her simply. 'She needs you now. Couldn't you pass up the assignment just this once?' she asked.

'When I'm inches away from worldwide success? What do you think?' Jen scorned. 'I'll be home when I'm good and ready, and I'll make it up to Adam then. And in the meantime I'd thank you to remember that he's mine, all mine, and that's the way it's staying.'

She rang off abruptly, leaving Denise holding the hand-set. She'd tried, she reassured herself, sighing heavily. She really had. But had she tried hard enough? she wondered. Had she been blunt enough? Perhaps if she'd told Jen the truth about Kate—the plain, unadorned truth—then surely she'd have changed her mind? Yes, that was it. Jen hadn't understood. Adam, being Adam, had simply given orders, and Denise had only hinted. But if Jen didn't know, did Denise have the right to put her in the picture? She shook her head. Somehow she doubted it, but short of asking Adam outright she was stuck.

'Roll on a week on Friday,' she murmured sardonically, reaching for a hairbrush. It really couldn't come soon enough.

* * *

'My dance, I believe.'

Denise flushed as Adam cut in, rescuing her neatly from a host of would-be partners.

They'd opened the dancing an hour or so ago, Adam's body unnervingly close to hers. It had been a tense ten minutes—Denise acutely aware of the glances that had followed them around, of the open curiosity on a host of smiling faces. 'Relax,' Adam had urged, sensing her unease. 'You're a five-minute wonder. The people who matter know why you're here, and those who don't aren't worth a thought. And the Press, I can assure you, haven't been admitted. Happy now?'

'Hardly,' Denise had countered tartly. 'But if you and Kate are, who am I to quibble?'

'Who indeed?' he'd mockingly echoed, and Denise had flushed, painfully aware that he was, in a gentle sort of way, making fun.

Now, cheek to cheek and shockingly aware of his hands on her body, Denise took the plunge. 'About Jen,' she muttered awkwardly.

'Jen who?' he queried with a hoot of derision. 'Jen the careless cousin, Jen the stunning model, or Jen the reluctant bride-to-be?'

'How about Jen the girl who loves you, Adam?' she tossed out softly.

Black eyes narrowed and Denise felt a *frisson* of unease. 'That subject's out of bounds, Denise,' he informed her curtly.

'Since when?' she demanded, tilting her chin and locking her gaze on to his.

He smiled grimly, ignoring the question, and as the music speeded up and the dance-floor crowded Denise was forced to let it go. Another five minutes passed before she was close enough to try again.

'Well?' she challenged simply.

'Well, what?' And the mocking smile told her she was wasting her time.

Swallowing a spurt of anger, she switched her approach. 'Jen rang,' she told him confidentially. 'You can tell me to mind my own business, Adam——'

'What an excellent idea,' he muttered evilly. 'Let's hope you take the hint.'

'You're not being fair,' she snapped. 'You kept Jen in the dark about Kate and expect me to take over at the drop of a hat——'

'And beautifully done, too,' he acknowledged, with another mocking smile. 'So what's the problem?'

'You are,' she told him vehemently. 'I've a life of my own, in case you've forgotten, and if Jen had all the facts, I'm sure she'd fly in tomorrow.'

'But she can't, can she?' he countered smoothly. 'And you're a fool, Denise, if that's what you're hoping. Jen can't show her face for the next two weeks—remember?'

'Only because you hadn't the sense to swallow your pride and ask her to stay.'

'I shouldn't need to ask,' he pointed out tightly. 'Jen should know.'

'Instinct, intuition or a crystal ball? Jen's only human——'

'And supposedly engaged to me. Hence the party, *engagement* party,' he niggled pointedly.

'Which Jen could have made, but for pig-headed you.'

'And how do you work that out?'

'Transport. Jen's in Milan, not halfway to Mars. Two or three hours and she could have been here. I assume you possess your very own jet?'

He smiled grimly. 'Irrelevant, Denise. Jen knew the score, and Jen made her choice.'

'Ah, yes,' she jeered. 'The arrogant Mr Walker or a glittering career. Tell me, how does it feel being second-best for once?'

His face darkened, his mouth a thin and angry line. 'Once, Denise, only once. You've hit the nail squarely. But never again, I promise you.'

'But I'm not the one you need to convince,' she countered sweetly.

The music hotted up again, the conversation lapsing, and when they next came together Adam had the anger under control. 'You look good,' he observed, an appreciative glance sweeping the length of her. 'That colour suits you. You ought to wear it more often.'

Denise flushed. 'My, my, a compliment from Adam. Sincere, I wonder, or just a clever ploy to change the subject?'

'Take your pick,' he entreated smoothly. 'You

wouldn't believe the truth if I carved the words in stone, so think what you like.'

'Thank you. I normally do. Like Jen, I've a mind of my own.'

'So it would seem. But luckily for me, that's the way I like it. You're quite a woman, Denise Elliot.'

'And you're quite a man—clever, manipulative and smugly convinced that I'll let you off the hook. Jen,' she reminded him as he raised a mocking eyebrow.

'She didn't want to come,' he reminded coolly. 'Despite the invitation.'

'But did you ask, or did you just assume?'

'And take the lovely Jen for granted? Maybe you're right,' he told her enigmatically. 'But it doesn't matter now, as long as someone does the job she glaringly left vacant. Worry not, Denise. I know you've a living to earn, but you won't lose out, I promise.'

'I'm doing you a favour,' she reminded grimly.

'And a favour done is a favour owing. You'll take what I'm paying, and then we're quits.'

'Keep your filthy money,' she snapped. 'I'm here under protest and believe me, Adam, I could walk out tomorrow and there'd be nothing you could do to stop me.'

'Be my guest,' he invited, with a sneering curl of the lips. He spread his hands expansively. 'In fact, if that's the way you feel, why wait? Go now. Go now, Denise Elliot, and may you rot in hell.'

'With you to keep me company? No chance.' She swung away, more hurt than angry, and, forcing her way through the noisy, laughing crush of people, headed for the walkway that led down to the terrace.

It was a beautiful night, cloudless and moonless, and the specially erected marquee glowed like a beacon. At the edges of the gardens lights had been installed, a fairytale effect that made it all seem unreal. But if the house and the grounds were enchanting, Adam's magic wand hadn't rested on its laurels. It was the dress that was the *pièce de résistance*—shimmering turquoise silk, low-cut and provocatively clinging, swirling out from the hip into a very full skirt. She'd felt like a million dollars for the first time in her life, and standing in front of the full-length mirror had ruefully admitted that Adam had been right. The shorter, bouncy hairstyle, highlights glinting gold, had softened the contours of her face and given unexpected depth to her cool grey eyes. But though Adam had noticed, Denise wasn't convinced his words were sincere.

She sniffed back the tears, hugging her arms to her body, aware of a chill in the air—more aware of the chill in her heart. Maybe Jen was right, she probed experimentally. Maybe she did feel more for Adam than she'd let herself admit. His devastating looks and aura of power were a potent combination and Denise was only human. Shame burned in her cheeks at the thought of Adam knowing. Yet what could he know? she silently argued. Oh, she *liked*

Adam, sure enough, despite the veneer of arrogance, but anything else. . . The sudden jolt of pain put an end to her wayward thoughts. Besides, she reassured herself, clutching at straws, it really was ridiculous.

Voices drifted near and she pulled herself together, heading for the shadows at the corner of the house.

'You have to hand it to Adam,' a feminine voice trilled. 'He sure knows how to throw a party. And I wouldn't have missed this for the world.'

'No,' her companion concurred with a faint American drawl. 'But Jen did and, seeing the way Adam's eyes follow that girl around, I wouldn't be surprised if Jen didn't live to regret it.'

'Don't be silly, Tom,' the woman scorned. 'Adam's putting on an act. He's mad about Jen, and everyone knows it. So when she does walk in, the acknowledged queen of the catwalk, Adam will be there, the proudest man in the world. And the girl is her cousin—the obvious choice to take Jen's place.'

'Exactly! Too obvious. And don't forget, I know Adam. We lived in the same part of town, remember? He adored Celeste, and since she died there's never been a woman who's lasted more than a month.'

'Apart from Jen.'

'Who just happened to appear at the right time and place.'

'What *do* you mean?' the woman queried coyly as Denise held her breath in the shadows.

'Simple, my love. If Adam's set on marriage, you can bet your bottom dollar there's a simple explanation.'

'Such as?'

'Oh—I don't know. Any one of a dozen things. Perhaps he wants a son and heir at last, or needs an attractive woman to help him entertain? But, after tonight, it's my bet he's found her.'

'Well, the girl's got something, I'll grant you that, but next to Jen?' A confident laugh rang out. 'No, Tom,' she insisted firmly. 'Adam's no fool, and he's not about to fall for second-best.'

They moved away as Denise stood and shivered, fighting back a fresh spurt of tears. She hadn't been meant to hear, she consoled herself, but it didn't draw the sting from the careless words. 'Second-best'. And it was true, all true; Denise *was* important—for now. Oh, Adam might have taunted, goaded, invited her to leave, but he had known she wouldn't go; she'd too much conscience to leave him in the lurch. No, she acknowledged bitterly. She was trapped.

'Oh, there you are,' Kate murmured anxiously when Denise wandered back into the crowded marquee. 'We'd been wondering where you'd got to, hadn't we, Adam?'

Denise raised her head to meet his gaze. I'll bet, she thought defiantly, but Adam simply smiled, offering an arm to Kate, inviting Denise to take the other.

'Come along,' he murmured silkily. 'It's time to eat. All this dancing has given me an appetite. And since the night's still young. . .'

Hours and hours, Denise realised woodenly. Hours and hours of smiling, dancing, making lively conversation with a host of perfect strangers, feigning happiness, craving love. Love! Oh, no! Adam could charm the birds from the trees when he chose to—but love? It couldn't be. And yet, the voice of common sense insisted, it explained such a lot—her confusion, the pain, her heated response to Adam's every word. And though the evidence was mounting, Denise closed her mind. Burying her head in the sand, maybe, but some things just didn't bear thinking about.

Half an hour later she was back on the dance-floor. Adam hadn't offered and Denise had been relieved, the glass of wine she'd downed with her meal soothing frayed nerves. The music slowed and Denise snuggled into her partner, her head resting on his shoulder. She could almost believe that she was happy, and the appreciative glances that strayed her way were balm to a battered ego. Among the dozens of laughing, simpering, expensively dressed women Denise could hold her own. Eat your heart out, Adam, she silently jeered. Denise Elliot doesn't need you, or your approval, to have a good time.

And then she saw him. Adam, the most striking man in the room, the white dinner jacket taut on powerful shoulders the perfet foil for the shock of black hair. Adam, cheek to cheek with a sleek and stunning blonde, his sultry eyes openly caressing. Adam, whispering words, sharing secrets, the woman's mouth curving into a warm, inviting smile. Denise went cold, the powerful surge of emotion taking her by surprise.

The music stopped suddenly and curious eyes turned to the dais where the orchestra played, and Denise felt a steel-like grip as Adam snared her wrist, sweeping her across the room and on to the stage.

'Smile,' he ordered tersely, teeth flashing white as they paused in front of the microphone. 'Ladies and gentlemen,' he murmured smoothly, and though Adam held the crowd, Denise seemed to struggle with the words. 'If I may propose a toast?' A waiter appeared as if by magic and Adam reached out, handing a glass to Denise before taking his own. 'To Kate,' he acknowledged brightly, holding his grandmother's gaze, 'a very special lady. And to Denise, a very *stubborn* lady, who's rashly promised to become my wife.' He raised the champagne. 'To the future—and whatever it may bring.' And, reading the truth about Kate in Adam's tender smile, Denise felt the sob rise.

'To the future,' echoed happily around them, and as the lump in her throat threatened to choke her a reassuring arm slid round her waist.

'Hey,' Adam whispered, hugging her briefly, the fleeting touch triggering ripples of heat. 'It's the happiest night of your life, don't forget. And Kate's,' he told her solemnly, black eyes gazing into hers and seeing to the centre of her soul. 'And you'll never know how much that means to me. Thank you.'

'I didn't have a choice,' she pointed out thickly, tears dangerously close.

'There's always a choice,' he told her enigmatically. 'I'm just glad you made the right one.'

The orchestra struck up as Adam swept her back into the crowd, dance after dance after dance, that left Denise dizzy with the pace and so completely caught up in a mass of whirling thoughts that she didn't notice when Adam swirled her out of the crush and on to the lawns.

'Come on,' he whispered huskily, his breath a warm flutter on her cheek. 'I've something I want you to have.'

An engagement ring! Oh, no! Denise froze. She'd been half prepared for a token, but not this, not this beautiful cluster of diamonds that was surely worth a fortune. What if it got lost—damaged? And she backed away, ignoring the ring, ignoring the hand that held it. 'No!' she muttered grimly, anger running in her veins. 'You're going too far. This farce has gone too far——'

'Not as far as I'm concerned,' Adam cut in harshly, and with the play of light behind him the angles of his face were carved out of stone. 'The ring belonged to Kate, was a gift from me when I made my first million. So, like it or not,' he chillingly informed her, closing in, a thrill of fear gripping Denise as she found herself backed against the wall, 'like it or not, you'll wear it—every second of the day while Kate is around—as a token of your love for Kate and for me.'

'Love for you?' she goaded recklessly. 'Oh, Adam, you really must be joking.'

'Am I?' he growled, a strange smile playing about the corners of his mouth. 'Well, in that case, Denise, I guess the joke's on me. Unless, of course,' he conceded softly, sure hands reaching out, gripping her shoulders, skin against skin, a gentle touch that scorched and soothed, scorched and thrilled, and turned her legs to water, 'unless, my little temptress, my lips can prove you wrong. . .'

CHAPTER FIVE

'No, Adam,' Denise protested feebly.

'Oh, but yes,' he insisted, fingers closing, holding, stroking, caressing, and drawing her imperceptibly nearer.

Denise went rigid as Adam's sultry gaze swept the lines of her body, his mouth curving in approval as he logged the generous swell of breast, the pinch of waist, the clinging contours of the dress—provocative, she knew, yet nothing like as revealing as Adam's response would seem to suggest. Closing her eyes, Denise dredged deep for the strength to resist, to rebuff.

'You want me, Denise,' he told her hoarsely. 'You can fight, you can resist, you can deny, but your body dances beneath my fingers and you come alive! Oh, yes,' he crooned, his mouth nuzzling hers, his exploring tongue mapping the quivering outline. 'You come alive. And you want me. Deny it if you must, but I know different, your body tells me different, and somewhere deep inside the truth lies, the truth you won't escape once I touch you, once I kiss you, once I taste your pert little mouth.' And he dipped his head again, the merest brush of the lips sending currents of heat swirling. Denise swayed dizzily, her arms moving upwards of their own accord, fingers entwining at the nape of his neck, Adam's growl of delight music to her ears as his mouth came down, hungrily, harshly, the pressure increasing as he met with her response.

Somewhere far away a voice was speaking, the voice of common sense, reminding her that Adam was playing games, that he'd take what he wanted with never a thought for the hurt he might cause, for the pain and devastation. But Denise didn't want to hear, closing her mind, refusing to listen, her body melting urgently, naturally into the straining lines of his.

'Oh, Adam,' she mewed as his mouth moved on, tracing the angle of her jaw with feather-like kisses that left a trail of devastation in their wake. And she moved her head from side to side as Adam moved down, lips caressing the column of her throat, branding and scorching, igniting, delighting, and she ran her fingers through the thick mass of hair, loving the texture, loving the tactile thrill of silk against her skin, shuddering afresh as Adam's hands began a tender exploration, shoulder to waist, his thumbs an erotic swirl of movement just below her breasts.

'Denise, oh, Denise,' he murmured throatily, his mouth moving on, lower, inexorably lower, until he was kneeling at her feet, his lips nuzzling the valley between her breasts, his tongue sliding over the trembling contours as his hands closed round, savouring the fullness, cradling the fullness, her nipples pressing shamelessly against the cupped palms. 'Oh, Denise,' he said again, indulgence threading the tone of passion. 'Your body doesn't lie. And your body was made for love, your body was made for me!'

Rustic benches dotted the terrace and Adam moved fluidly, swiftly, taking a seat and urging Denise on to his lap where he quickly claimed her mouth again, his tongue sliding through into the moist, inviting sweetness, lips now gentle, now demanding, his mouth against hers, his mouth part of hers, and Denise glowed, pulsed, came alive, wonderfully alive, the pleasure enslaving, the rest of the world ceasing to exist as Adam taught her body how to love. It was magic, pure magic—the touch, the taste, the exquisite torment—and Adam's response was every bit as shocking as her own, the knowledge unbelievable. He wanted her! He needed her! Adam Walker might taunt and tease and mockingly deride, but he wasn't as indifferent as he'd have her believe. He wanted her, and her heart soared.

Tiny shoestring straps slid from her shoulders, magic fingers caressing the creamy curve of skin, the skimpy bodice staying in place heaven alone knew how, and Adam's mouth plundered hers as his hands glided across her body, scorching, searing, branding, fingers brushing the swell of breast, brushing, teasing, teasing the flimsy silk, coaxing the folds away from Denise's heated flesh, the hiss of indrawn breath the sweetest music ever made as her swollen breasts spilled over, Adam's hands closing round, urgent thumbs teasing the straining nipples.

His lips had claimed her mouth again, lips and tongue creating havoc, hands wreaking havoc, every touch, every taste unbelievably right, the knowledge that Adam wanted her, needed her an intoxicating potion that drove the world and all it stood for far, far away. Until Adam pulled away, the unmistakable flash of triumph in sultry black eyes.

Denise froze. He was playing with her. He was using her. He was simply making a point, and the surge of elation died. 'Ten out of ten,' she awarded frigidly, sliding from his lap and folding her arms protectively across her naked breasts. She faced him defiantly, shivering—part rage, part shame, part cold, she acknowledged as the goose bumps appeared—and the eyes that lashed him were heavy with contempt. 'Ten out of ten,' she said again, with a sneering curl of the lips.

'As good as that?' he challenged lazily, the mocking smile deliberately insulting.

'But of course,' she swiftly derided, choking back the tears. 'After all, you're hardly short of practice, hey, Adam?'

'You don't say,' he drawled, but the mouth that scoffed no longer feigned amusement. 'And which particular bird has been twittering out of turn?' he asked.

'So many?' she queried softly. 'Too many to know, too many to remember?' She shook her head in silent condemnation.

He shrugged. 'It's none of your damn business,' he castigated coldly.

'Isn't it?' she smiled grimly. 'Well, that's where you're wrong. *You're* my business. Everything you do, everything you say, each and every nuance of expression is part of my life for the next two weeks, and if you don't like it, you've only got to say and I'll be gone. But if I stay—*if*, Adam,' she emphasised softly, 'then these cosy scenes stop now. That—or I leave.'

'You're threatening me.'

'No, not threatening.' Denise shook her head. 'Simply stating facts. I'm here for a reason, a special reason, and I'll do my best to carry the role Jen has forced me into. But make-believe or not, we go by the rules.'

'So?' His arctic gaze pinned her.

'So—you play ball; I play ball. You rock the boat; I jump overboard. Simple.'

'Oh, I *see*.' He leaned back against the uprights of the bench, folding his arms, seemingly relaxed, just the angles of his face chiselled out of granite. 'Who'd have guessed it?' he observed sneeringly. 'The kitten has claws, and she's not afraid to use them—as long as she's got the upper hand. Except, of course,' he tossed out calmly, 'she's wrong.'

'Is she?'

'Yes, Denise. Very wrong.' He raised a hand, fingers loosely clenched, black eyes fastened on her face. 'One——' the index finger flexed '—no one, but no one, threatens Adam Walker. Two—this might be a game, but make no mistake about it, *I* make the rules. And three——' He paused, an evil smile playing about the corners of his mouth, and as Adam prolonged the suspense Denise went cold, hugging her arms to her body in an effort to keep out the chill. She was dying inside—the shame, the pain almost more than she could bear, yet she wouldn't let it show, wouldn't give Adam the satisfaction of knowing how much he'd hurt her. Only Adam, clever, mocking Adam, seemed to know. He smiled—the satisfied smile of a cat sure of its kill. 'Jen,' he prompted softly, slyly, insidiously. 'Hit out at me and you hit out at Jen—the goose that lays the golden eggs,' he pointedly reminded her. 'No Jen, no money, no studio, no business. Oh, yes,' he emphasised, lips twisting cruelly, 'I'll make sure of it. The greedy little cousin will have blown it.'

Smiling again, he swung himself upright, towering above her, and a nervous Denise stumbled backwards, the sudden flash of teeth eloquent proof that he'd caught her reaction, was openly amused, and she cursed herself for betraying fear. Adam wouldn't touch her now if she were the last woman on earth, and the anger surged afresh, draining away as he paused, reaching into a pocket.

'Your move,' he explained, placing the small square box on the table between them, black eyes pools of poison. 'Wear it, Denise,' he commanded coldly. 'After all, you haven't any choice. Not according to the rules.'

It was a difficult few days, Kate's sharp brown eyes missing little, and though Denise did her best to seem her normal cheerful self, something must have shown.

'I could be speaking out of turn,' Kate began, with a reassuring smile, 'but at my age, Denise, I'm allowed a little licence. Tell me, is there something on your mind?'

'Adam. Plans for the future. You,' Denise replied carefully, knowing that Kate would see through any evasions. And besides, she was speaking the truth.

In public Adam was nothing but attentive, the ever-loving fiancé, but once they were alone everything changed—oh, nothing she could fault, but the veneer of manners simply masked the contempt. And as for Kate, she was all too aware of what the next few weeks could bring. Denise barely knew the older woman yet already felt the love that radiated from her. As Adam had said, Kate was special.

'Silly girl,' Kate admonished gently. 'I wouldn't have come if I'd known you'd be upset.'

'But I'm so glad you did. And think of Adam. He loves and needs you and the party wouldn't have been the same if his special lady hadn't been there. You couldn't deny him that, now could you?'

Kate laughed. 'I could never deny him a thing, and it sure was hard at times. But it was worth it. And when Adam bought me that ring I was the proudest woman in the world. I'm proud now,' she added softly, warm brown eyes fastened on Denise. 'Proud of you both and so proud to see you wearing a special token of Adam's love. Thank you, Denise.'

'Oh, no!' Denise gulped, glancing down, seeing

the ring through a blur of tears, and she jumped up, hugging Kate fiercely. 'Thank *you*,' she said simply. 'For everything.'

Kate's expression sobered suddenly. 'You really do love that boy of mine, don't you, Denise?'

'Very much,' Denise replied simply. And the white lie hurt. It hurt like hell.

Surprisingly, things improved when Kate went into hospital.

'Why not go home for a couple of days?' Adam suggested over breakfast. 'You must be bored with nothing to do, and with your business standing idle you must be losing clients. I'll run you back now, if you like.'

'And miss seeing Kate?' Denise shook her head. 'I'll stay—if the lord and master doesn't mind, that is?'

His mouth tightened. 'No, the lord and master doesn't mind,' he told her evenly. 'I was thinking of you. Kate would understand, Denise. And the last thing she needs is to be treated like an invalid.'

'I wasn't going to treat her like an invalid,' Denise needled, reaching for the coffee-jug. 'Besides, Kate wouldn't allow it. Like me, she's a very stubborn lady. Perhaps that's why we hit it off so well.'

Adam smiled. 'You're probably right. I wonder why I hadn't noticed how alike the two of you are? And yet Kate's such a gentle person, things going her way without so much as a frown.'

'The iron fist in the, velvet glove,' Denise explained sweetly. 'A clever woman is like a first-class rider—she prefers the lump of sugar to the whip.'

'And has the man, like the unsuspecting horse, eating out of her hand, I suppose.'

'Exactly! I couldn't have put it better myself.'

Adam grinned, taking the dig in good part. 'I'm going into Birmingham,' he said instead. 'Why not come with me? You could wander round the shops for an hour and meet me for lunch before we visit Kate. And if the Walker World doesn't appeal to madam's fastidious taste, there's a first-class burger bar just around the corner.' Amber lights danced in laughing black eyes. 'And if madam plays her cards right,' he teasingly informed her, '*she* can foot the bill.'

'With an offer like that,' Denise replied pertly, 'how could a girl refuse? Thank you, sir. You've got yourself a deal.'

Kate had some news.

'It's looking good,' she explained, with an air of suppressed excitement. 'It's too early to be sure, but the signs are optimistic, and I've a feeling in my bones that this time I won't be disappointed.'

'When will you know?' Adam enquired casually.

An alert Denise was attuned to the strain. He was smiling, but the expression in his eyes was guarded.

'Friday afternoon when they've finished all the tests. Which reminds me. Don't be surprised if I'm groggy tomorrow. The anaesthetic's bound to leave me sleepy and it might be better if you both stayed at home.'

'No chance,' Adam insisted firmly. He reached for her hand, cradling it gently, Kate's dainty fingers strangely vulnerable in Adam's generous palm, and, watching them, Denise felt the sudden sting of tears. It wasn't fair, she inwardly railed. Why should someone as lovable and loving as Kate have to go through the pain and inconvenience of the tests only to face an even bigger challenge—an operation that might not be successful or that other stark alternative that Denise couldn't bring herself to name?

The door opened, a cheery face peering round. 'Good afternoon, Mrs Walker,' the girl trilled, dragging a heavily laden trolley in her wake. 'Sweets, chocolates, drinks, magazines? You name it, I sell it. Or would you rather have a paper? I've one or two left from this morning.'

'No, thank you, dear,' Kate replied brightly. 'I never read the English papers. They're always so boring—nothing but politics and sport. I'll have a couple of magazines, though. Any will do, whatever's left.' Adam paid the girl, who placed the glossy magazines on the bed, blushing fiercely as she backed herself out of the room. 'And unless my eyes deceived me,' Kate added slyly, 'Adam's made a conquest.'

'But luckily, Kate,' Adam countered cheerfully, 'I've only got eyes for you—and Denise.' He turned his head, the mocking gaze meeting hers, holding hers as Denise parried the scorn with her own brand of defiance.

'Oh, look,' Kate broke in, unaware of the tension crackling on the air. 'She's the image of Denise. Isn't that strange?'

Oh, no! Denise closed her eyes for a fraction of a second, not wanting to believe, not wanting to face the truth. Jenny. In Technicolor glory, splashed across the cover of the top magazine. And as her eyelids fluttered open she caught the flash of pain on Adam's rigid face and knew the game was over. And Kate, poor Kate, would be so hurt.

'Jenny Elliot,' Kate added doubtfully into the screaming silence. And then she smiled, brown eyes full of dancing lights. 'So *that's* where I'd heard the name before. Jenny Elliot, Denise Elliot. She models clothes; you model clay. No wonder I got confused. You *are* related?'

'My cousin,' Denise explained, awaiting the barrage of questions. It never came, Kate flicking idly through the magazine before holding it out for Denise. 'You take it, dear,' she murmured wearily. 'I'm too tired to read and it's a lovely souvenir for you to keep. And when I'm feeling up to it you can tell me all about your jet-setting cousin.'

'Thank you,' Adam murmured later, his hand on her elbow as they headed for the car.

'For what?' Denise enquired carefully, achingly aware of his touch and of a new respect shining in his eyes.

'For coping,' he said simply. 'For telling the truth. For managing not to overreact. Anyone else would have given the game away.' And, raising a hand to his mouth, he kissed two fingers which he lightly pressed against his lips. 'Thank you,' he said again solemnly, and as Denise continued to stand, wide-eyed and mute, he dipped his head, brushing her mouth briefly, searingly, shockingly with his own.

They collected Kate on Friday, the expression in her eyes a curious mix of hope and apprehension. 'They're giving me time,' she explained calmly. 'To talk things over and make up my mind. And if I do decide to go ahead, the operation's scheduled for a week today.'

A week today. Denise swallowed hard. Seven short days and her job would be over. Adam wouldn't need her. Whatever the outcome, Denise would be free. With luck Kate would pull through, and with an extra year ahead of her Adam could risk the truth. Kate, being Kate, would forgive the deception, and Denise would be alone again, would slide back into the old life, a life without Adam— uneventful, undemanding, but meaningless and empty.

'Come on,' Adam urged, his strong arm cradling Kate's tiny waist. 'Let's go. If I know you, the decision's already made and you'll be back here soon enough. Let's go home and you can tell us all about it.'

It didn't take long, the traffic being light once

they'd left the city behind, and Denise sat with
Kate, talking, listening, reminding herself that she
was supposed to be happy, smiling till her cheeks
ached, and all the time watching Adam—the crop
of hair that brushed the back of his collar, the
haughty profile, the angular planes of his face. Long,
tapering fingers gripped the wheel, the tiny hairs on
the backs of his hands hinting at the mass that would
cover his chest, deliciously inviting, wonderfully
enticing, and she had to drag her wayward thoughts
away from other erotic reminders, erotic desires,
consoling herself that if life without Adam would be
empty, it would be easier too. It was much too
disturbing, this churning emotion that Adam managed to provoke without trying, and Denise couldn't
wait to get her life back to normal. No more
pretending, no more putting on an act. She'd be
losing a lot in more ways than one, but she'd be
getting back her peace of mind. Or at least, she
amended sickly, that was what she was hoping.

Kate touched her hand as the car cruised to a
halt. 'Home,' she said simply. 'And I can't begin to
tell you how good it feels to be here with you and
Adam.'

Denise smiled, reaching across and hugging, holding, shockingly aware of how fragile Kate really
was, and she blinked back the tears as she followed
her inside.

'I think I'll go to my room,' Kate explained
apologetically. 'It's been a long day, and if no one
minds I need to lie down for an hour.'

'I'll walk you upstairs,' Adam insisted, leaving Denise to her thoughts—troubled thoughts that grew sadder by the moment. It was a long and lonely twenty minutes and then Adam was back, and, logging the grim set of his mouth, Denise went cold.

'What is it?' she asked, stumbling to her feet and hurrying to meet him. 'For God's sake, Adam, tell me what's wrong.'

'It's Kate,' he said simply. 'She's worried about the operation. She's got it fixed in her head that she won't pull through and she wants the wedding brought forward.'

'You're mad!' Denise went hot then cold in the space of half a moment, her reeling mind struggling to cope with Adam's terse words.

'No, Denise,' he countered curtly, the tiny pulse at the corner of his mouth drawing her gaze. 'Believe me, I've never been more sane—or more serious.'

Serious? She smothered an hysterical giggle. How could he stand there and quietly announce that he'd set the wheels in motion, that he'd already made the phone calls and that the wedding was set for Thursday afternoon? And she moistened her lips with her tongue as she struggled to stay calm.

'We can't,' she said starkly, moving about in a daze of distraction. 'An engagement's one thing, but a wedding——'

'If Kate wants a wedding,' Adam insisted, 'Kate gets a wedding. Simple.'

'Not to me,' Denise replied tersely. 'And it's my life——'

'Wrong,' he reminded her harshly. 'It's Kate's life.' And he smiled grimly, heading for the drinks tray and pouring two large brandies.

'You're mad,' she said again, taking the glass he offered without conscious thought.

'So you keep saying. But a bargain is a bargain—unless your word counts for nothing?'

'I agreed to an engagement,' Denise insisted, taking a long, hard sip of the fiery liquid and barely noticing the kick. 'A phoney engagement.'

'Wrong again. You stood beside me on that dais while two hundred guests toasted the future bride and groom. *You—Denise* Elliot—promised to marry me.'

'But it was a sham,' she protested, a note of hysteria creeping into her voice. 'A pretence. You know it and I know it.'

'But Kate doesn't,' he pointed out calmly, black eyes holding hers, refusing to allow her to look away. 'Subject closed. The wedding goes ahead if I have to drag you kicking and screaming every inch of the way.'

He didn't wait for a reply, probably didn't expect one, she realised bitterly as he crossed to the window and pushed aside the blinds.

It was a glorious May afternoon and Adam's house was a slice of paradise—the terrace, the lawns, the carefully tended flowerbeds—yet Denise was locked in hell. The sun was shining on the river and everywhere was calm—except inside her heart, inside her mind where turmoil reigned. To marry Adam, to be his wife yet not his wife, wanting, needing, always needing, was too cruel to suggest, too cruel to expect and yet Adam—arrogant, handsome, powerful Adam—had calmly assumed that Denise would do it. The anger surged.

She moved, darting across, every fibre of her body quivering with emotion. 'Oh, no you don't,' she told him harshly, tilting her chin, whipping his face with the fury of her gaze. She stood squarely before him, hands on hips, eyes shooting flames. 'This is my life you're arranging without so much as a second thought. *My* life, *my* future. Only, you can't. I won't let you. Are you listening, Adam?' she demanded frigidly. 'You'll have to think again. You'll have to tell Kate the truth. And if she still wants the wedding, the answer's simple. Find Jen. Drag *her*, kicking and screaming every inch of the way, which is what you should have done in the first place instead of putting us through this ridiculous charade. I quit—as of now.'

'You can't.'

'Can't I?' she rasped, heading for the door. 'Just you watch me.'

The venom in his tone stopped her dead. 'That's right, go! Turn your back. Forget me. Forget Kate. And may you and your conscience rot in hell. But you'd better make the most of it,' the evil voice entreated. 'After today you're living in the real world—with Jen.'

She spun round, eyes dark with horror, and Adam smiled, a chill smile of triumph.

'Ah, yes,' he almost purred. 'I thought that would stop you. All that lovely money,' he sneered. 'Jen's money. Take care, Denise, that it doesn't just slip through greedy fingers. Jen's too,' he added matter-of-factly. 'Still——' He paused and the vicious gaze travelled the length of her, down then up, the contempt so fierce she could barely hold her ground. 'If Jen's not used to living on the breadline, she'll learn. She'll have to, hey, Denise?'

'You wouldn't dare,' she breathed. And yet instinct told her that Adam would. A snap of Adam's fingers could shatter Jen's dream. No career, no world title, no Adam. Oh, yes, Denise had worked that out. Zak was the man on the spot but Jen was shrewd enough to keep her options open—as long as Denise didn't rock the boat.

'Wouldn't I?' He smiled again, then spread his hands expansively. 'In that case, my dear, there isn't a problem. Goodbye, Denise.' And he turned away, seemingly unconcerned, subject closed. Denise could have been a million miles away. She simply wasn't there as he flung himself down on the sofa and reached for a book from the nearby table, flicking idly through the pages.

Denise didn't move. She couldn't win. Whatever she decided, she just couldn't win. Walking out on Adam meant walking out on Jen, and yet the alternative didn't bear thinking about.

'Still here?' he enquired without glancing up.

'Forgotten the way home? Or do you need to borrow the cab fare?'

Denise swallowed hard, biting back the tears, the scathing retort on the tip of her tongue. How cruel he could be. Arrogant and cruel—and ruthlessly determined to have his own way. For Kate, she consoled herself. He was doing it for Kate, and yet it didn't help. She was damned if she did and damned if she didn't—as long as Adam was playing devil's advocate.

It was her turn to head for the drinks trolley and she measured out the brandy with fingers that shook. She spun round, cradling the glass in her hands, swirling the golden liquid round and round as she struggled to find the words. She took a long, hard gulp, and as the spirits hit the back of her throat sensed Adam's interested stare. Quick as a flash she switched her gaze, steel-grey eyes colliding with his. The moment was timeless. And then Denise broke the deadlock.

'Very well,' she conceded, with a defiant thrust of the chin. 'You win.' And she raised the glass in awful parody of a toast. 'Here's to the happy couple,' she mocked. 'And may you and *your* conscience rot in hell.'

CHAPTER SIX

'THANK you.'

It wasn't the words, the softly spoken, totally unexpected words that hit her. It was the expression in his eyes. Steeled to parry triumph and scorn, the shock of Adam's pain caught her unawares. Something awful crossed her mind.

'Oh, Adam,' she breathed, hardly daring to say it. '*You* don't expect Kate to come through either, do you?'

He didn't reply, simply sat and stared unseeing into the distance, and Denise moved, leaden feet carrying her forward. She knelt at his feet, wanting to help, needing to help, yet powerless to know where to start.

A lifetime passed before he glanced down. 'I don't know,' he said simply, his whole expression bleak. 'I honestly don't know. God knows, Denise, four months wasn't long, but it's a hell of a lot more than seven short days.' And the anguish and the pain were more than she could bear.

'You're wrong!' she insisted emphatically, willing herself to believe it. 'You're wrong. Kate will come through. She's a fighter—like you. Believe it, Adam, you must believe it. For Kate's sake. Think, Adam, think. If Kate saw you like this——'

'She'd probably tan my hide,' he admitted, a ghost of a smile crossing his features. 'And I'd probably deserve it. Man of means or ragged rascal, it's the same Adam Walker underneath.'

'Was it really so dreadful?' Denise probed, sensing a way to channel the pain, divert troubled thoughts.

'I didn't think so—then. But the snotty-nosed boy grew up, went to school, saw other kids with moms and dads, toys and sweets—and a shirt for every day of the week. There was a whole new world out there and I wanted to join it, take Kate away from the drudgery. She worked her fingers to the bone, cleaning, scrubbing, taking in washing. Anything to help feed me. And now the money doesn't matter. Don't you see?' he asked in torment, wild fingers ruffling his hair, the dishevelled effect unwittingly appealing. 'I'd give it all away tomorrow if it would help keep her safe. Only it won't. The money can't help, nothing can.'

'Strange,' Denise mused, searching her mind for a lever, something, anything—anything to stop the punishing thoughts. 'I'd never have taken you for a loser.'

His head snapped up at the softly spoken words, the flash of anger in coal-fired eyes the most welcome sight in the world.

'That's more like it,' she approved wholeheartedly, and as the truth slowly dawned on Adam's glowering features Denise allowed herself a smile.

He grinned ruefully, leaning back into the cushions, the lines of his body much more relaxed. 'You're quite a fighter yourself,' he observed. 'The school of hard knocks must have a lot to recommend it. So——' black eyes shot her a shrewd, assessing glance '—it's all set?'

'So it would seem,' Denise replied carefully. And then something struck her. 'What about Jen?'

'What about her?'

'She'll have to know,' she reminded him.

'Then she can wait and find out—the hard way.' He smiled grimly, daring her to contradict him. 'Fair's fair,' he pointed out coolly. 'Jen walked out, Jen can take the consequences. All part of the price of success.'

And with that chilly pronouncement, Denise had to be content.

It didn't stop her fretting, though, the worries and the doubts continuing to niggle. Jen wanted Adam—wanted that world title too, and with the verdict due before the end of the week the next few days would be crucial. If Jen took the crown, Denise sensed unerringly, she'd be back, expecting her reward. And if the decision went against her. . . Denise went cold. Whichever way she viewed it, it didn't make the prettiest of pictures.

As it turned out, her worries were groundless.

'Jen's been offered a job in the States,' Adam explained when the news broke. 'She'll be back when she's ready to face the British Press, and what's more she'll do it in style. I'll make sure of it.'

'You?' Denise asked, wrinkling her brow. And

then the penny dropped. Jen's consolation prize. A
high-profile tour of America, all expenses paid—
courtesy of Adam Walker plc. A clever distraction? she couldn't help wonder. Or the gift of a man
in love?

She swallowed hard and, closing her mind to the
truth, picked up her book, hoping Adam would take
the hint and leave. It was peaceful in the library—
Adam's library, she grudgingly admitted—and she
resented the intrusion. Kate was resting and, with
Adam engrossed in the Sunday papers, Denise had
seized the chance to slip away. Only now he'd
tracked her down, was watching, waiting, black eyes
far too knowing, the shadows beneath them catching
at her heart. It was worry about Kate, she consoled
herself, not wanting to believe that he was fretting
over Jen.

Adam shrugged. 'There's something you ought to
read,' he explained, dropping a newspaper into her
lap and turning away. 'Page six. Then bin it. I know
Kate doesn't bother with the papers, but I'd rather
not run the risk—not this week.'

She found it at once. 'Millionaire on the
Rebound', ran the headline, and she winced, guessing what was coming. 'International businessman
Adam Walker, apparently jilted by the woman he
loves, is finding consolation in the arms of her
double. In fact Mr Walker's on/off romance with
top model Jenny Elliot has taken a most unusual
twist recently. As our diary can exclusively reveal,
the rich and handsome Adam Walker is shortly to

marry. And the name of the lucky bride-to-be, you may be wondering? Denise Elliot. Yes, folks, no prizes for guessing. Not only a Jenny Elliot look-alike, but Jenny Elliot's little-known cousin. A simple matter of keeping it in the family, perhaps?'

There was more, most of it salacious gossip, and Denise crumpled the sheets in disgust. Sadie Graham, she wouldn't mind betting, hoping the woman would have the sense to stay away from the wedding. If she spoiled Kate's day there'd be no holding Adam. And, though Sadie Graham was freelance, Adam Walker was a powerful not to mention dangerous man to cross.

Thursday. Her wedding-day. Denise felt chilled, though the afternoon was sunny. She wore a suit, an off-white linen two-piece, the skirt a demure inch and a half above the knee. And though she tried her best to sparkle, the face beneath the froth of a hat was pinched and pale.

'Relax,' Adam entreated as they reached the Town Hall steps. 'Smile. Look as if you're enjoying yourself. It's the happiest day of your life, don't forget. And Kate's no fool. Smile, for heaven's sake. Smile.'

She flushed, darting a glance at Kate's happy profile. Adam was right. If Kate could appear serene with her future far from settled, why couldn't Denise? Only it wasn't easy with a million and one things playing on her mind—Jen, the absence of reporters, the needles of doubt that refused to go away. But most of all Jen. And though Adam was convinced that Jen was in the States, Denise wasn't sure. Her cousin was unpredictable at the best of times and, with her pride in shreds, could still turn up to ruin Adam's careful plans.

Only Adam, self-assured, confident Adam, was right and Denise breathed a sigh of relief once it was over.

The next few days were equally strained—Kate's hospital admission, the nerve-racking hours while Adam paced the corridors, a caged tiger full of suppressed emotion, and Denise, torn apart with anguish but powerless to help. Then the surgeon's face as he walked towards them, Adam's relief, the explosion of joy.

'Come on,' he whooped, hugging Denise, swinging her round to the indulgent smiles of the other visitors. 'We'll take a peep at Kate and then we'll stay in town. Tonight we're going to celebrate.'

It was nothing like as fraught as the last time she'd stayed in one of Adam's plush hotels—two weeks ago, she realised, amazed at how much they'd packed into a short space of time. And now it was almost over. Kate had been handed a new lease of life and Denise was redundant. Jen would make her peace with Adam and wedding-bells would ring—for real this time—and they'd all live happily ever after. Except Denise. The country cousin would slip on her mousy mien and blend into the background. Work, work, nothing but work. A cold and empty life without the man she loved. Oh, yes, she admitted belatedly, the pain scything through, she loved him. Had probably loved him all along.

And yet, she acknowledged, hungry eyes devouring the clear-cut features, the generous mouth, the lightly tanned skin, nothing could be worse than sharing a house, sharing a meal, sharing time—yet always aching for a love she'd never be entitled to. Adam absent might be hell, but a flesh and blood Adam barely aware of her existence was too cruel to endure.

'Something wrong?' he enquired as her urge to eat faded. 'If the steak isn't cooked enough——?'

'No. It's fine. Everything's fine,' she insisted, and she smiled brightly across, heading off the probing questions. He sees too much, she realised, logging the expression in strangely tender eyes. And though Adam might guess, he'd never know for sure, not unless she gave herself away. And then she'd have his pity. Oh, no, she vowed, swallowing hard, hating each and every exquisite mouthful. Never that.

'Brandy?' he suggested as they moved into the lounge bar. 'Or would madam prefer a vodka? A dash of tonic, a slice of lemon and lots and lots of ice,' he supplied, word-perfect and teasing as he, too, recalled that first evening.

'Vodka would be lovely,' she agreed, and when the drink arrived swirled the cold, clear liquid round and round the glass as she waited for Adam to raise the subject of the future. Only he didn't, sitting opposite, saying nothing, watching, waiting, taking occasional sips of brandy, black eyes strangely brooding. The silence and scrutiny were too much for ragged nerves.

'So——' she began carefully. 'Everything's settled. I'll move out in the morning, if that's all right?'

'Why?'

'Isn't it obvious?' Denise almost snapped. 'You don't need me any longer and I've a business to run, in case you've forgotten. Multi-millionaire I'll never be, Adam, but I do need to earn a living.'

'I'm paying for your time,' he pointed out slyly. 'And if it isn't enough to cover your losses, the answer's simple. Submit a fee. Name your price. I couldn't be fairer than that, could I?'

'And I've told you, I'm doing you a favour. No,' she pointedly amended, 'I'm doing Jen a favour, and since Jen's coming home——'

'Is she?' he asked, breaking in, a strange smile playing about the corners of his mouth. 'What on earth gave you that idea?'

Denise went white. 'Two weeks, Adam,' she pointed out coldly. 'As far as I'm concerned anything else is overtime, and that's down to Kate. And since Kate no longer needs shielding from the truth——'

'Oh?' He drained his glass and signalled for another, his eyes never leaving her face. 'And how do you work that out?'

'Kate's getting better——'

'Exactly!' He leaned forward, the movement swift and urgent. 'Think, Denise, think. Have some sense. Kate *will* get better, but we must give her time. Shock her now and heaven knows how it would affect her. Could you live with that?' he demanded tersely. 'Could you live with your conscience if something happened to Kate? Can you afford to take the risk?' he added slyly. And then he paused, spreading his hands in eloquent invitation. 'Well?'

Denise swallowed hard. Moral blackmail. He'd tried it before, had used Jen to twist her arm, but that wouldn't work now. Denise had kept her part of the bargain and now she was free—technically. Only Adam, clever, clever Adam, had baited the trap, would use her love and concern for Kate to get his own way. And, glancing across, she caught the knowledge in his eyes and knew that Adam had never doubted it.

'You're playing God,' she told him simply. 'And no one, not even you, has that right.'

'So you'll stay?' he insisted, ignoring the barb, the supreme confidence galling.

'I haven't any choice, have I?' she needled. She held his gaze. 'Six weeks. Six weeks convalescence, the surgeon said. And then I'll walk away. And this time, Adam, you'd better believe it.'

'For Kate, six weeks is a lifetime,' he pointed out. And then he smiled, strange lights glowing in the depths of his eyes. 'I'll probably never say this again, but I'll say it now, and then you can remind me as often as you like. You may be a very stubborn lady, Denise Walker, but you're a special one, too. Don't ever change, will you?'

Denise felt the tears rise. She picked up her glass, draining the contents before scrambling to her feet. 'I'm going to powder my nose,' she murmured thickly, needing to escape.

Denise Walker. She took her time, splashing her cheeks with cold water. Denise Walker. It sounded so right, so good—her name linked with Adam's, her name on Adam's lips. Yet it was nothing but a sham. A shell. A convenient piece of fiction. The sob rose, choking, Denise making a superhuman effort to pull herself together as the door behind swung open. She went cold, her startled gaze colliding with another in the glass.

'Ah, the blushing bride herself,' Sadie Graham drawled, with a sneering curl of the lips. And then her expression changed. 'What's this?' she enquired gleefully. 'Have the lovebirds had their first tiff? Or has Adam just discovered he's married an imposter?'

'Mind your own business,' Denise retorted coolly, amazed at the woman's knack of arriving out of nowhere. First London, now here. Unless, she realised sickly, the reporter was shadowing Adam, biding her time before turning out another scurrilous piece. She made to push past, pulled up sharp by an unexpected grip on her arm, and, glancing down and seeing the vividly painted talons, the anger surged. 'Let go of me,' she entreated frigidly, shaking free. 'And in future keep your hands, as well as your crude insinuations, to yourself.'

'Dear me,' Sadie mocked. 'Things are looking

bad. But you know what they say, don't you, Denise? Marry in haste, repent at leisure. And it *was* an indecent dash to the altar.' She paused, dropping her eyes to Denise's slender waist, a gleam of speculation in sly green eyes. 'Now, why, I wonder?'

Denise flushed. 'You're wrong.'

'Am I?' The older woman smiled. 'Well, only time will tell, and then there'll be another Walker brat demanding his place in society.'

'Say that again,' Denise insisted icily. 'Say that again, and I'll make sure Adam drags you into court so fast your feet won't touch the ground.'

Sadie's smile broadened. 'He'd never make it stick,' she purred, and then she leaned across, each and every word dripping poison. 'You see, my dear,' she explained confidentially, 'slander's only slander when someone's telling lies.'

Denise pushed past, taking huge gulps of clean, fresh air as she crossed the foyer. The woman's lying, she told herself, clinging to the thought. She's lying. And besides, she consoled herself bitterly, it was nothing to her. Adam's private life was his concern.

'What is it?' Adam asked at once, a worried frown creasing his brow.

Denise couldn't speak, too choked to say the words, and she turned her head, Adam's eyes following the line of her gaze. He whistled sharply under his breath and Denise went rigid as a reassuring arm came round her shoulder, the touch of skin on skin almost more that she could stand.

Dipping his head, he whispered, low and urgent, 'I'm going upstairs and you're coming with me, and with that evil woman watching every move, we'll do it in style—won't we, my love?' And he kissed her, briefly, searingly, shockingly. 'Won't we?' he said again, smiling down into the soul of her. And Denise nodded, love and pride coming to the rescue.

'You bet!' she agreed, with a defiant toss of the head, and, linking her arm with his, smiled brightly up into laughing black eyes as they swept in triumph from the room.

The air of bravado lasted less than a minute. 'Hey,' Adam chivvied, tucking a hand beneath her chin and forcing her to meet his gaze, 'she isn't worth a thought. She's poison, pure poison, and I should have banned her years ago. I'll do it now,' he tagged on grimly. 'And make sure she never sets foot again on Walker property.'

'And give her ammunition?' Denise shook her head. 'She's the lowest of the low, and as long as we ignore her there's no way she can touch us.' Or at least, she added silently, that was what she'd like to believe. But the stark truth was that Sadie Graham's vile remarks refused to go away.

With time on her hands Denise turned to work and a growing pile of orders, and though she had meant to move home while Kate was in hospital Adam out-thought her, the contents of the studio appear-

ing lock, stock and barrel overnight, housed in the
workroom Adam had commissioned.

'You'll wear yourself out,' he pointed out frankly,
arriving late to find her working. 'And it's not as if
you need the money.'

Denise straightened, pushing a lock of hair out of
her eyes and smearing clay across her cheek. As
usual at the sight of Adam her heart skipped a beat.
The laughing eyes, the surprisingly tender smile
when Adam chose to use it and the powerful physique were a potent combination, and the longer she
was with him, the harder it would be to leave.

'So you keep saying,' she acknowledged, turning
back to the bowl she was shaping. 'But there will be
life after Adam Walker, and if my business folds
now I'll be left with nothing. It's a temporary
arrangement—remember?'

His mouth tightened. 'How could I forget when
my unwilling wife never wastes the chance to
hammer the point?' He dragged at his collar, loosening the tie, the dishevelled effect strangely appealing. 'And talking of wedded bliss, has it never
crossed your mind that as the ex-Mrs Walker you'll
be worth a small fortune when this is all over? No,
I didn't think it had,' he observed as her chin
snapped up, jerking fingers ruining the almost perfect bowl. And, having dropped his bombshell, he
gave a shrug of pure indifference and strolled lazily
into the night.

'Damn, damn and damn the man,' Denise muttered evilly, snatching the lump of clay and flinging

it vehemently at the door. Barely pausing to wipe her hands, she marched boldly across the lawns, into the house, up the magnificent marble staircase and, without stopping to think, swept unannounced into Adam's room.

Disconcertingly, he wore little more than a smile, the towel round his waist barely adequate, and Denise stopped short.

'Do come in,' he drawled sarcastically. 'Would madam care to take a seat?' And he nodded at the bed, meaning plain.

'No, madam wouldn't,' she snapped, her face on fire. 'Madam isn't stopping.'

Adam merely shrugged, dropping on to the covers with scant regard for modesty, and Denise was forced to tear her gaze away from the long legs with their covering of hair, growing more and more confused as she raised her eyes, past the towel that stayed in place heaven alone knew how, to the powerful chest and the thick, dark mass that nature intended fingers to plunder—her fingers, she decided absurdly—and on again, colliding at last with laughing black eyes.

'Well?' Adam drawled, velvet voice threaded with amusement.

'Well! Is that all you can say? You walk in, calmly drop a bombshell and then saunter out. What the hell do you think you're playing at?' she demanded, and though *she* glared down at Adam, the advantage stayed his.

He raised a lazy eyebrow. 'Payment for services

rendered,' he explained. 'It's written into the contract you signed. Oh, nothing so crude as a pre-arranged sum, but every wife's entitled to a cut and this time, Denise, the grateful husband intends being generous. Unless of course——' he paused, smiled, then patted the bed '—unless you'd like payment in kind?'

'You really must be joking,' she spat. 'I wouldn't want you if you were the last man on earth——'

'No?' Adam moved, and with a lightning flick of an arm he'd snared Denise, iron fingers circling her wrist, and the more she struggled, the more Adam smiled, the nearer he tugged her. 'No?' he said again, and, 'Dear me, what a blow to my ego. My loving wife prefers my money to my charms.'

'Oh, no, she doesn't!' Denise protested hotly, and then she realised what she'd said.

The sly smile widened. 'Well, well, well. So the truth slips out. And in that case, Denise, this marriage really could be convenient—for both of us.'

'Don't be so insulting!' With a vehement tug she freed her hands, eyes shooting daggers as she stood her ground. 'I don't want your money and I won't share your bed. I'm here for Kate, and don't you forget it.'

'And talking of Kate, she's coming home tomorrow, so I'll be moving in with you for the rest of her stay.'

'She is? Oh, good!' And then the lightly spoken words sank in. 'What did you say?' Denise asked, suddenly cold as ice.

'If Kate's coming home, we need to share a room,' Adam explained. 'It's what Kate would expect, and in the eyes of the law we are man and wife.'

'No!' Denise backed away as Adam swung himself upright. 'No,' she said again, shaking her head. 'No. No. No!'

'Oh, but yes,' he contradicted starkly. 'I'll have Maria move my clothes first thing tomorrow.'

'But you c-can't, she stammered. 'It wouldn't be right, it wouldn't be fair, it wouldn't be——'

'Fun?' he slipped in softly, moving slowly yet surely in her direction. 'Are you sure?' he almost purred, locking his gaze on to hers, the strange compulsion in turbulent depths creating havoc in her mind. 'Are you sure you'd rather sleep alone, all alone in that huge feather bed that was simply made for love?' And he smiled as he drew near, much too near, the powerful body cutting off the means of her escape. A nervous tongue moistened her lips as Denise reacted to the nearness, to the sheer masculine presence, the tanned skin glistening from the shower, the clean, healthy smell—Adam's special smell.

He simply oozed temptation, the urge to touch, to taste, to kiss and be kissed so overpowering that Denise felt faint, and she smothered a groan as she closed her eyes, blocking out the man but not the need. She wanted him, oh, how she wanted him, but Adam was simply playing games, filling time, amusing himself, and Denise refused to become just

another toy. Adam could seek his pleasure somewhere else because Denise had drawn the line. And
though her body screamed out for satisfaction, her
mind stayed in control.

Adam moved close as Denise inwardly squirmed.
She was caught fast against a chest of drawers, her
eyelids flying open in alarm as Adam touched her,
not with his hands, not with his mouth, but leaning
forward from the hip and pinning her, the shock of
his arousal, the shock of her response, sending
currents of heat swirling through her body.

'You want me,' he growled huskily, black eyes
openly caressing, lingering on the swell of breast
beneath the clay-smudged blouse. 'You want me.
And I want you, Denise. So why deny ourselves the
pleasure?' And he dipped his head, lips brushing
hers briefly, searingly brief, his arms either side of
her shoulders, not touching, not restraining, simply
denying. Her body screamed out to feel those arms
around her, to have his lips exploring hers, his
tongue entwined with hers, his body part of hers,
and her legs turned to water at the thought.

She slumped against him, the piteous mew in the
back of her throat an eloquent plea for mercy, and
Adam growled, scooping her into his arms and
striding forecefully to the bed. He placed her gently,
almost reverently among the pillows, his eyes never
leaving her face, his expression solemn, smoky,
heavy with desire, and Denise smiled, the tremulous
smile of a woman in love, a woman about to receive
love, and Adam's mouth softened.

'I want you,' he said simply. 'Every day for the past four weeks I've wanted you. And now you're mine, all mine. I'm going to make you mine. Understand?'

And she nodded, no longer hearing the words, simply seeing the man, wanting the man, needing the man. Adam's hands caressed her body, his mouth against hers, and she parted her lips, eyes shining, body eager, as he lazily snapped the straining buttons of her blouse, one by one, top to bottom, exposing the tiny wisp of bra and then he paused. He raised his eyes, naked desire smouldering in their bottomless depths, and Denise smiled shyly up at him, wanting, needing, trusting, knowing Adam would be gentle, would teach her body how to love. She wanted him, and Adam, wonderful, powerful, exciting Adam wanted her!

And then she sobered. He wanted her. Nothing more, nothing less. He didn't love her, didn't need her. But arrogant Adam Walker wanted to possess, to make her his own. And what Adam Walker wanted, Adam Walker got. Only not this time.

'No!' she insisted harshly, pushing forcefully against his chest. 'No, Adam, no.' And she slid from beneath his body, scrambling from the bed as his face darkened, tightened, storm-clouds gathering in frigid black eyes.

With a muttered oath he swung himself upright, his magnificent naked body never more appealing, never more taboo, and he lashed her with his eyes as he whipped her with his tongue. 'No one, but no one plays games with me, Denise,' he frigidly informed her. 'And I give you due warning. You want me. You might not want to believe it, but everything about you is hungry for love. It's written loud and clear in your smoky grey eyes and every touch, every taste underlines the craving. You want me. And next time there'll be no mistake. Next time you'll want me so badly that you'll beg. And maybe, just maybe,' he tagged on tersely, 'I'll teach you what you've been missing.'

He turned away, heading for the shower, the incident over, indifference oozing from the pores of his skin. Reaching the door he turned, his eyes flicking over her, the interest fleeting, transient, almost insulting, and then he smiled, a cruel and calculated sneer of the lips.

'Goodnight, Denise,' he drawled provokingly. 'Sleep well, won't you? And you'd better make the most of it. As from tomorrow, you're sharing your bed with me.'

'Really, Adam?' she queried silkily, crumbling inside but damned if she'd let it show. 'Well, have I got news for you, Mr God's-gift-to-women Walker. Sharing a room we may be,' she acknowledged bitterly, 'but make no mistake about it, *you're* sleeping on the sofa.'

'In my own house?' he challenged coolly. And then he laughed. 'Good try, Denise, but to borrow a phrase, you really must be joking.'

CHAPTER SEVEN

IT WAS hell—Kate's company a godsend, Adam's absence at work a tangible relief. And Denise was glad to escape to the studio, catching up on orders yet finding time for Kate. They'd sit on the terrace and watch the river swirling by, catching the occasional drift of voices or a hand raised in greeting, and hour by hour, day by day, Denise would see an improvement. Kate was growing stronger and in a week or two, three at the most, Kate had every intention of moving on.

'But I'll be back,' she reassured them one sunny afternoon when Adam arrived early and joined them for tea. 'I've set myself a goal, and though it's just a hope, the dream of a selfish old lady, who knows? If nature takes its course, I might see that great-grandchild yet.'

'Oh, Kate!' Denise filled up at the thought and she didn't need to glance at Adam to know his lips had tightened. Foolish, foolish dreams, she realised bitterly, and it wasn't only Jen's neck she felt like wringing. She couldn't fault his motives, but how she wished he'd been honest from the start.

Adam poured the tea. He raised his cup. 'It isn't quite champagne,' he explained, with a tender smile for Kate, 'but I guess it will do. Here's to nature,' he toasted simply, and he turned his head, eyes bottomless pools as they rested on Denise.

She swallowed hard, returning the gaze unblinkingly. It wasn't nature Adam should invoke but a miracle. And then she went cold as something crossed her mind. Oh, no! She almost dropped her cup. Even Adam couldn't hope to talk her into that.

'Don't even think it,' she told him later in their room—oh, yes, he *had* moved in, in theory at least, she acknowledged mockingly, conscious of Adam night after night just a few feet away in the dressing-room.

'It was—just a thought,' he tossed out calmly. 'An idea. But the decision would be yours. I've twisted your arm enough as it is. And Denise——' he moved across to cradle her face, the brush of his thumbs both tender and unnerving '—I really am grateful. But when Kate leaves at the end of the month you're free to go—if that's what you want.'

'Oh, yes?' The rawness of the pain goaded her to sneer. 'And supposing I change my mind? Supposing I stay? Supposing I crawl into your bed, Adam—just to make Kate's dream come true. What happens then? To me? To the child? Don't be so naïve,' she derided, twisting free of the disconcerting grasp. 'The idea's absurd.'

'But not impossible,' he pointed out slyly.

'No, I don't suppose it is, given your casual approach to life.'

'And what's that supposed to mean?' he enquired dangerously.

'You know. Don't pretend you don't. You're a

normal healthy male and you've had more than fun. And that sort of fun, Adam——' She halted, Sadie Graham's gibe festering in her mind, but she couldn't say the words, couldn't think how to phrase it.

'Do go on,' he entreated silkily. 'You're a woman of the world, don't be coy. I've played around, is that it, been careless with my favours? That *is* what you're implying, isn't it, Denise? That somewhere along the way the love-them-and-leave-them Adam Walker must have sired a bastard?'

'It—had crossed my mind,' she admitted, flushing.

'And is that what you believe?'

'What I believe doesn't count,' she told him primly. And when Adam didn't react, but simply stood impassive, she found herself saying impatiently, 'Of course I don't belive it. You're too close to your own years of hell to put a child through that.'

'So what's the problem?' he enquired, mouth set hard, the mocking smile absent.

'You are!' she shouted. 'With your mad ideas. And no, I can't fault your motives. But Kate would understand, she's strong enough to take it—now. Tell her, Adam, tell her the truth.'

'I'll tell her when I'm good and ready.'

'Why?' she demanded hotly. 'Why not explain— about me, Jen, everything? Kate's going to live. And though she's flying home, she'll be back. Think, Adam, think. Every time she phones, every time she writes she'll ask about me, hint about a baby.

She's got to know. For weeks, months—yes—you could have carried it off, but they've given her a year. It won't work. Can't you see, you've got to tell her the truth.'

'No,' he insisted harshly. 'It's too soon. Much too soon.'

'Suit yourself,' she retorted tightly, turning away. As Adam had said, she was almost free to go. And then what Adam chose to say or do would be none of her concern.

'So you see,' Kate explained apologetically, 'it's just a minor setback and perfectly normal according to the doctor. But it looks as if you're stuck with me. Just another month, if you're sure you don't mind.'

'Mind?' Adam's face changed, delight spreading out across the well-loved features. 'Kate, my shrinking violet, do you really need to ask? We'd be thrilled, wouldn't we, Denise?'

His eyes held hers across the table, features impassive yet the message plain. She couldn't hurt Kate, he was silently reminding her and the anger burned. How could he doubt her? she inwardly fumed, but she wouldn't let the hurt show.

'If it makes Adam happy,' she told Kate simply, 'then I'm happy too.'

Two weeks. Six weeks. Another month. She ought to feel trapped yet it didn't seem to matter. Her time with Adam would be over soon enough, and though life would be easier, there was bound to be a void.

'Thank you,' Adam murmured in the privacy of their room, eyes warm as velvet. 'You've given a lot, and don't think I don't know it.'

'What did you expect?' she tossed back curtly, the fact that he could doubt her continuing to sting. 'Kate's special. You don't know how lucky you are spending your childhood with someone who loved you, really loved you. You needn't worry, Adam, I wouldn't hurt Kate for the world.'

She turned away before he could reply, pointedly heading for the shower. Forced to share a room—or almost, she bitterly amended—they'd developed a set routine. Denise would shower first and, safely wrapped in a soft towelling robe, would slip on to the balcony to read. Luckily the evenings had been dry. She dreaded to think what she'd have done had the weather been unkind—cowered under the bed-clothes, she witheringly supposed. And, with Denise engrossed in her book, it would be Adam's turn to shower.

Twenty minutes later she checked her watch. Eleven-fifteen. Adam had promised to be out of the way by eleven but, ever-cautious, Denise tended to linger. She strained her ears, catching nothing but silence, and, deciding to finish the chapter in bed, tiptoed inside. All was quiet and the tell-tale pencil of light under Adam's door was missing. She was safe—though from what she didn't stop to ask. And then the shower-room door swung open.

'Y-you startled me,' she stammered as the book

slipped through nervous fingers, landing noisily on the floor. 'I thought you'd be in bed by now.'

'So I gathered.' Generous lips twitched with amusement. He leaned against the doorjamb, folding his arms, black eyes openly caressing. 'Sorry, Denise. I popped down to the library for some papers I'd been working on, and instead of locking them away did another half-hour. But you needn't worry,' he reassured her drily, 'I'll only be a moment, and to spare your maidenly blushes, I am more or less decent.'

Decent? In that scrap of a robe? And colour flooded her cheeks as derisive thoughts took a swift erotic turn. To cover the confusion, she dived for her book, colliding head-first with Adam who'd had the same idea.

'Hey, steady on.' Strong arms reached out, catching at her shoulders, fingers closing round as the tremors began.

Denise closed her eyes, blocking out the room, the man, but not the need, that all-consuming need to lie in his arms, to kiss and be kissed, to have his body part of hers. It wasn't fair. She loved him, wanted him, needed him, and yet Adam could never give her what mind and body craved. And she'd tried so hard not to love him, to keep him at a distance, putting up barriers, prolonging the niggles, yet still he managed to creep under her defences. It just wasn't fair, and in another few weeks he'd forget all about her—could well be back with Jen, she realised sickly, Jen, her beautiful, selfish cousin, who took what life offered with never a backward thought—for Denise, Adam, Kate, even the hapless Zak Peters.

Adam moved, her thoughts of Jen vanishing as he swung her into his arms, holding, cradling, so close she could feel the reassuring thud of his heart against her cheek, her emotions spiralling out of control as Adam laid her gently on the bed.

'Don't,' she whimpered pleadingly, eyes fluttering open as he lay down beside her. 'Please, Adam.'

'Hush, sweetheart,' he reassured her softly. 'I simply want to touch, to taste, to kiss. I want to hold you, I want to kiss you. And that's all, sweetheart. That's all, I promise. Unless you want more,' he added thickly, his gaze locking with hers and seeing to the centre of her soul.

Denise didn't reply—how could she with Adam's body close, Adam's eyes stripping her bare? And she nervously licked her dry lips, the pink tip of her tongue unwittingly inviting. Adam groaned, an anguished sound from somewhere deep inside as he gathered her roughly to him, his mouth seeking hers, lips hungrily devouring, Denise freezing for a fraction of an instant, her mind holding out as her body reacted with a life of its own, that first touch of Adam's mouth banishing the fears.

Her arms slid round him, hands holding, caressing, impatient fingers fumbling at the fastening of his robe; she craved the tactile thrill of skin on skin and, sensing the frustration, Adam raised his head, smoky eyes heavy with promise as he shrugged himself free. Denise smiled, a shy, tremulous ray of sunshine that broadened as Adam, too, smiled a tender smile before dipping his head, the tip of his tongue tracing the outline of her lips, Denise moaning aloud as Adam tugged her close.

'Denise, Denise, Denise,' he crooned against the corner of her mouth, sensually caressing the contours of her face. Feather-like kisses rained down on fluttering eyelids, the touch enticing, igniting, Denise whimpering with pleasure as Adam's mouth explored—nibbling, scorching, soothing and scorching; his lips nuzzled the hollow at the base of her neck, then lower and lower, inexorably lower, his hands slipping round, urgent fingers tugging at the fastening on her waist.

There was a pause as the robe fell open, his sharpe intake of breath a wondrous indication that he found her body pleasing, and, bathed in the glow of those coal-fired eyes, Denise almost purred. Adam wanted her! Adam needed her! And the knowledge was simply out of this world. Adam wanted her!

She reached out, a single, tentative finger touching his mouth, tracing the outline, his lips parting as he took possession, teeth gently biting, tongue lapping, the sensation strangely erotic, and then his mouth was nuzzling the palm, Denise gurgling deep in her throat as Adam raised his head, the velvet eyes seeking hers brimming with emotion.

'You're very beautiful, do you know?' he asked solemnly. And when Denise didn't reply he said again hoarsely, 'You're very beautiful, Denise. Believe me, you are.'

He tasted her mouth, and her mind screamed out for more—for Adam's fingers caressing her burning body, for Adam's mouth branding heated skin. And yet still he denied her, the frustration growing like a fever.

'Please, Adam,' she murmured against the nibbling lips. 'Please, Adam, please.'

'Hush, sweetheart,' he said again, huskily, indulgently. 'We've all the time in the world, my love. I want you. I've wanted you for so long. I tried so hard to do without you, but every minute, every hour I was fooling myself. I want you. And now that I'm close to tasting your body, making your body part of mine, I want everything right, everything perfect, and I want *you* to want *me* every bit as badly. And then, and only then, will the moment be right. Understand?'

She nodded, eyes brimming with emotion, too choked to reply, too near the state of perfect happiness to object to the delay, the waiting itself exquisitely painful, exquisitely right, and she slid her arms around his neck, bringing his head down to hers slowly, savouring the moment, postponing the moment of contact, Adam's growl of pleasure music to her ears as the control snapped. Adam wanted her, oh, how he wanted her! And the knowledge was out of this world. And yet, common sense reminded her cruelly, that was all. He wanted her. He didn't love her, didn't need her, and if the truth were known, that promise to Kate lay behind the urge to make her body part of his.

She froze.

The probing fingers halted, Adam's eyes darkening, a flash of pain and anger replaced by disbelief. He swore softly, eloquently under his breath as he swung himself upright. And then, equally softly, he asked simply, 'Why, Denise, why?'

'You're doing it for Kate,' she said bitterly. 'Not for me, not even for yourself. And I refuse to be your brood mare.' Yet, seeing the hurt, feeling the hurt and needing to soften the blow, she added almost pleadingly, 'I'm sorry, Adam.'

'So am I,' he retorted thickly, the muttered words so low she wasn't sure she'd heard them. He moved quickly, fluidly, proudly, footsteps muffled in the thick pile of carpet, and Denise couldn't watch as Adam left the room, the faint click of the door announcing that she was alone—never so alone.

She crumpled, slumping into the pillows, the tears dangerously close. She'd wanted him, oh, how she'd wanted him, and the temptation to reach for the cup of happiness had almost been too much. It didn't seem fair. In the eyes of the law they were man and wife and yet they didn't belong. Denise was playing a part, she reminded herself. And as for Adam? She swallowed hard. She just didn't know any longer, but she'd be a fool to pretend that he'd never wanted Jen.

She moved slowly, wearily towards the shower, her skin tingling from the touch of Adam's hands,

Adam's mouth, Adam's body, and though water couldn't wash away the memory, it would be a start. Drawing level with his door, she paused, aching, wanting, needing, and without conscious thought reached out, trembling fingers closing around the handle.

He was sitting on the bed, his back to the door, dejection written into every line, and Denise halted, afraid to move, almost afraid to breathe. Adam might not want her. He was a proud man and he was hurting inside. He wouldn't be used to rejection and the need to wound in turn would gain the upper hand. He'd hit back. He'd whip her with his eyes, lash her with his tongue and then he'd take his own sweet revenge. *He'd* reject *her*. Oh, yes, she knew that Adam could reject her, but that was a risk she just had to take.

'Adam?' she said softly, the single word shattering the silence.

'What do you want, Denise?' he asked without turning.

She licked her lips, moving forward, all the things she had wanted to say sticking in her throat. And then she stopped. It was no good. She shouldn't have come, shouldn't have laid herself open to his scorn. Had she no pride? she asked herself. Had she no shame? Throwing herself at a man who'd use her, who'd take what she was offering and then when Kate flew home would toss her aside with barely a second thought. But though the truth hurt, it didn't seem to count. She had to try, and if

Adam's response was inevitably linked to pleasing Kate, hers wasn't. She loved him, and that was all that mattered—for now.

She drew close, so close, and then she paused, allowing the robe to slip from her shoulders. Time stood still. Everywhere was silent, just her pounding heart drumming in her ears, drowning out thought, driving away the doubts. And still Adam ignored her. Moistening her lips with a nervous sweep of her tongue, Denise moved slowly, infinitely slowly, reaching out, tentative fingers closing on his shoulder.

'Don't,' he said thickly as the shudders convulsed him. 'Don't touch me, Denise, not unless you're prepared for the consequences.' And when Denise didn't move, didn't speak, but simply began to caress the warm, inviting skin, he added in anguish, 'Hell, woman, I'm only human, and there's a limit to what I can take.'

'Take me,' she said simply, shamelessly, kneeling behind him, her naked breasts thrusting into the contours of his back. 'Take me, Adam.'

CHAPTER EIGHT

ALL too soon came the phone call.

'Jen! When did you get back?' Denise asked delightedly, and then something struck her, the pleasure fading fast. Jen back in England meant Jen back in Adam's life.

'A couple of days ago,' her cousin told her airily. 'Don't you read the papers? I was front-page news in most of them.'

'Sorry, Jen. I haven't seen a paper in weeks. I've been too busy.' Work, Adam, Kate—the demands on her time seemed endless. And, of course, Adam vetted any news that could upset Kate.

'So I gathered,' Jen observed with a touch of asperity. 'Which is why I'm calling. You and I need to talk. I'll meet you for lunch,' she instructed coldly. 'Twelve o'clock sharp at the Walker World. And Denise,' she cautioned frigidly, 'don't let me down.' Denise felt her heart sink. Jen was annoyed, which was understandable really, but then the anger surged. How dared she? Jen had walked out; Jen could share the blame. And if she *had* come back for Adam, she'd just have to wait. Denise smiled grimly. As long as Kate was around, Jen didn't stand a chance.

Leastways, that was what she'd have liked to

believe. Catching Jen's smug expression ninety minutes later, Denise faced the truth. She was kidding herself. Still, she wasn't about to let Jen know and, bracing herself for the worst, she crossed the crowded restaurant.

'My, my, someone looks happy,' her cousin drawled slyly as Denise slid into a chair. 'Marriage must suit you.'

Denise flushed. She was late, aware that she'd taken her time in a subconscious need to put off the moment, and as nervous fingers reached for her wine, she mulled the suggestion over. Happy? Yes, or as happy as she'd ever be with Jen casting shadows on her marriage—a marriage in name and deed now.

After their night of pleasure she hadn't known what to think, and, waking early, gently cradled in Adam's arms, all the doubts and fears had come back to plague her. Adam would reject her. She was sure Adam would reject her. Hadn't he made his point, she berated herself, brought Denise to the point of begging? And the tears had formed, squeezing out between her lashes, trailing silently down her cheeks. And then Adam had opened his eyes, wonderful eyes glowing like coals, and she'd known. It was going to be all right. Everything was going to be all right.

Only now, reading the scorn on Jen's exquisite face, Denise felt something die. She was a fool. The marriage was a sham. So she and Adam shared a bed. That wouldn't last once Kate moved on, and she'd better not forget it. No, Adam and Jen belonged together, and Denise was achingly afraid that it was only a matter of time.

'So,' Jen began abruptly, uncaring of the soup cooling on her plate. 'These are the thanks I get for taking you under my wing. While the cat was away, the mousy little cousin seized the chance to play—with Adam.'

'Look, Jen, I can explain——'

'Skip it, Denise, I've already been told. Told, you understand. Not asked or consulted, just told that Adam was getting married—to you.'

'But he didn't have a choice,' Denise protested urgently. 'Adam wanted you, needed you, and since you weren't here——' She broke off, searching for the words, for a hint of a thaw on Jen's stormy face. She didn't get one. 'Can't you see?' she pleaded softly. 'He did it for Kate.'

'Ah, yes, Kate.' Jen smiled grimly. 'The doting grandma. She's recovering well, from what I've heard, and in that case, Denise, your days with Adam are numbered. You'd better make the most of it,' she observed cruelly. And then her expression changed, a gleam of speculation in sly blue eyes. 'But there again, judging from the glow in your cheeks, you're doing just that—hey, Denise?' She leaned forward, the air of grave conspiracy a calculated sham. 'Tell me,' she invited softly, 'how's the happy husband? Not making too many demands, I hope?'

Denise squirmed. She'd never lost the annoying

habit of blushing under pressure, and with Jen's sharp eyes missing nothing lying would be futile. 'Adam's—the perfect gentleman,' she murmured awkwardly.

'How very disappointing,' Jen mocked. 'He's not pining for me, by any chance?' But she didn't wait for a reply, patting Denise on the arm. 'Never mind,' she consoled. 'He's bound to notice you sooner or later. It's only a matter of time. And once he hears my news, well——' There was a loaded pause, eloquent shoulders carelessly hunching. 'Who better to console him than the blushing bride herself?'

'News?' Denise queried, apprehension prickling.

Jen's sly smile spread out across her face. 'I knew you hadn't noticed,' she purred. She held out her hand, her left hand, the enormous sapphire and the diamonds catching at the light. 'Well, aren't you going to congratulate me? Zak popped the question, and of course I said yes. We're making it official on my birthday.'

'You're getting engaged?' Denise said stupidly. 'But that's impossible. You want to marry Adam.

'Only I can't, can I, Denise, since Adam's already hitched—to you.'

'But I don't understand—it doesn't make sense.'

'On the contrary, my dear, it makes perfect sense. Call it my consolation prize—or the price Adam has to pay for crossing me.'

Denise gasped. 'You mean, you're using Zak to

hit back at Adam? But that's—that's—that's inhuman,' she ended weakly.

'Is it?' Jen wrinkled her pert little nose. 'Well, maybe you're right,' she agreed off-handedly. 'But what the head doesn't know the heart can't grieve for, and Zak won't lose out, I promise. And once Adam's free——' She paused, shrugged, then spread her hands expansively. 'Who knows? I might even be prepared to take him back.'

And break another foolish heart, Denise realised bitterly. Poor Zak. He had no idea of how things really stood, or the lengths to which Jen would go to salvage her pride. And as for Adam. . .she swallowed hard. 'Listen, Jen——'

'No, Denise,' her cousin cut in harshly. '*You* listen. You're to blame for this—falling in with Adam's every plan, first the engagement, then the wedding. And, yes,' she hissed as Denise tried to head her off, 'I know about Kate. But I've had enough. It's gone too far. It's my career you're ruining between you. I'm a laughing-stock. *Me*, Jenny Elliot, a laughing-stock, and why, Denise, why? Because Adam couldn't wait. Only, two can play at that game, and then we'll see how Adam enjoys a taste of his own medicine.'

The waiter approached as Jen finished speaking, and imperious hands waved him away. 'Forget lunch,' she instructed crisply, crumpling her napkin into a ball and tossing it on the table. 'The mood I'm in now, food would choke me, and besides, I'm watching my weight. One frump in the family is more than enough.'

Denise blinked back the tears, struggling for control, Jen's naked scorn almost more than she could bear. Adam's mine, the flash of ice-blue eyes reminded her. He might have married you, but it's all a matter of time. And Denise sat locked in silent misery as Jen searched for her keys. Palming them neatly, she paused, lips twisting in awful parody of a smile.

'I almost forgot.' She drew a slim, expensive package out of the clutter and placed it on the table. 'I've brought you this. Zchenni. It's an original. Named after me and specially created by a top French perfumier. We're launching it at next month's Paris collection. Until then, I'm the only woman in the world wearing it. You see, Denise,' she explained with a muted hint of triumph, 'I've almost reached the top, and when I do, the world will be my oyster. And as for Adam, well——' There came another elegant, eloquent shrug. 'He'll just have to wait and see, won't he?'

With a rustle of silk she swept from the room, hips swinging jauntily, uncaring of the stir she caused among the lunchtime diners.

Alone and forgotten, Denise slumped into her chair. She reached for the box, the heady scent of musk catching at her throat. It was—distinctive—she acknowledged ruefully, just like Jen, and much too heavy for Denise. And yet she understood the gesture. This is me! Jen was stating publicly, and though Denise would take the fragrance home, she knew she'd never use it.

'There's something on your mind, isn't there, my dear?'

Denise felt the blush rise. She'd been lost in thought, completely unaware of the older woman's scrutiny.

'Sorry, Kate. I was miles away. Problems with an order,' she hastily explained and, crossing her fingers at the tiny white lie, forced a reassuring smile. 'But there's plenty of time,' she added brightly. 'It isn't due out until the end of the month, and if it isn't right by then it never will be.'

The end of the month. Kate's farewell, and a day or so later Jen's shock announcement. And Adam's pain as his world fell apart. And Denise? What about her world? she asked herself bitterly. Did anyone care about her?

'If there was something bothering you—only if, mind,' Kate soothed, 'you wouldn't have to keep it bottled up. I've a lifetime of listening behind me, and I promise my lips would be sealed.'

Denise swallowed hard. 'Thank you,' she said simply, meeting those wise brown eyes with difficulty, Adam's eyes, she achingly acknowledged. But she couldn't confide. Not in Kate, not in anyone. The clock in the hall chimed three. 'What shall we do about dinner?' she asked instead. 'Adam said not to wait, but the last time he drove up from London he didn't stop to eat on the way.'

'Why not put it back an hour?' Kate suggested sensibly. 'And if he hasn't arrived by then, we'll go ahead without him.'

Denise nodded, going off in search of Maria. She'd won the housekeeper over at last, the prickly exterior hiding a heart of gold. Maria adored Adam, would go to the ends of the earth to please him and, having judged Denise and read more than Denise intended, she'd visibly thawed.

'Let's make it special,' Denise began. 'Salmon and asparagus mousse, beef in filo pastry and your *pièce de résistance* for dessert. We'll show Adam what he's missing when he puts business first.'

'If I know Adam, it won't be the food he's missed these past few days,' Maria murmured knowingly, and Denise went pink. Maria *could* be right, but Denise was horribly afraid that it was just wishful thinking.

Eight o'clock came and went, an anxious Denise resisting the urge to wander to the window. A watched pot never boils, she sternly reminded herself. Adam would arrive when he was good and ready, and wistfully gazing at the long, empty drive wouldn't help at all.

Maria appeared in the doorway.

'Come on,' Denise insisted, linking Kate's arm. 'We'll make a start. Adam could be hours yet, and I for one am starving.'

She led the way to the elegant table set glaringly for three, Denise rapidly losing her appetite. The telephone rang as she reached for her napkin.

'No prizes for guessing who this is,' Kate observed as Denise half rose. And then she sat down, knowing Maria would take the call and afraid to raise her hopes. Besides, if Adam was ringing now, the reason was plain. Another night away, another night alone. Or leastways, she amended swiftly, she'd be alone. How Adam filled the time, she'd rather not face.

Maria reappeared. 'That was Adam. He wouldn't let me disturb you, He'll be late and you're not to wait up. If he's hungry he'll raid the fridge.' She sniffed, disapproval heavy in the sound. 'I'll leave something out just in case,' she added dourly, shuffling back to the kitchen.

'Never mind,' Kate consoled over-brightly. 'He's on the way, and that's the main thing.'

On the way? An hour and a half's drive from London and he was on the way? Oh, no. Denise choked back the tears. Whatever Adam was doing for the next couple of hours, driving home he wasn't.

Midnight. Not a sound, not a creature stirring. Only Denise, pacing the floor of her room. If she'd checked the time once in the past half-hour she must have done it a dozen times, and she flung herself down on the bed, reaching for her book. She'd read, pass the time more sensibly, and for the next twenty minutes she really did try. Reaching the end of another uninspiring chapter, she dropped the novel on the floor and, fastening her robe, wandered out to the balcony. She'd watch for the lights, for the powerful beam of Adam's car, and if he didn't come home in the next ten minutes she'd take herself off to bed. She wouldn't sleep, she was sure of it, but at least Adam wouldn't be annoyed to find her waiting up.

She checked her watch again. Time up. No Adam. No peace of mind. Denise sighed. She climbed on to the duvet, drawing her robe snugly round. Five more minutes, she promised herself, and then she'd try to sleep. And then she heard a noise, her straining ears not quite certain, the thumping of her heart drowning other sounds.

She was up in an instant, reaching the door as the handle turned. 'Adam!' she cried delightedly, pitching forward. He scooped her into his arms, his smile wide as he swung her round and round, Denise felt dizzy, partly from the twirl, mostly from the heady feel of Adam's body close, and she raised her face, lips parting in silent invitation, and Adam's throaty growl filled her with heat as he hugged her fiercely, his mouth claiming hers with all the fire and hunger four days' separation could create.

'Miss me, honey?' he asked, the threads of laughter music to her ears.

'Whatever gave you that idea?' she teased in turn, but she pulled back, suddenly shy under Adam's knowing gaze. She'd be giving herself away, reacting so wantonly, so naturally, and she backed away, perching on the edge of the bed, hungry eyes fixed on Adam as he moved about the room.

'Perhaps I should go away more often if this is the

welcome I get.' And he pulled at his collar, loosening the tie, black eyes openly caressing. 'Five minutes,' he promised smokily, shrugging off his clothes. 'And then I'm all yours.'

Five minutes. Denise smiled, excitement rippling through, and, hearing the sound of running water, felt the need to freshen up as well. She'd run a comb through her hair and dab some perfume on her pulse-spots, and she glided across the room, retrieving Adam's shirt and trousers on the way. A handkerchief fluttered to the floor, a delicate wisp of lace, and she froze. It wasn't Adam's and it certainly wasn't hers, and the urge to ignore it, pretend she hadn't noticed, almost gained the upper hand. Only she couldn't. She had to know. One way or another, she simply had to know. And then she realised, the pain scything through her. It was the perfume, that unmistakable smell of musk.

Oh, Jen, how could you? she silently screamed, crumpling the handkerchief into a small ball and going out on to the balcony. Think, she urged herself. Think. Stay calm. Say nothing. It could be something perfectly simple, perfectly innocent. Only, knowing Jen, Denise wouldn't bank on it. Revenge? she wondered fleetingly. The sting of hurt pride? The need to hit back at someone—at Denise—for Adam's public defection. Oh, yes, she'd worked it out exactly. And there wasn't a single thing she could say or do. And then she stiffened, the surge of anger masking the pain.

'Had a good trip?' she enquired sweetly when a

damp and glowing Adam emerged from the shower.
He wore a towel round his waist and for this she
was grateful, but even so her traitorous body reacted
to the sight. Folding her arms defensively across her
aching breasts, Denise raised an eyebrow.

'It was just business,' Adam informed her easily.
'And yes, it did go my way in the end. But it was
quite a fight,' he added when Denise didn't repond.
'And I rarely had a moment to myself.'

'No, I don't suppose you would,' she agreed, her
lips tightening at the thought of Adam and Jen
together. Adam and Jen, a cosy little twosome.
Adam and Jen sharing a meal, sharing a moment,
sharing a bed. And then Adam crawling home to do
his duty—for Kate. She almost laughed. Poor
Adam. Forced to marry Denise because the woman
he loved was halfway across the world, carving out
a name for herself. And then losing out to another
man with influence— if he only but knew it. He
thought he'd got it made, yet he could end up with
nothing. No Jen, no Denise. But pots and pots of
money, she remembered. Adam's consolation prize.
All that lovely money.

'Is something bothering you?' He was standing in
front of the mirror, running a comb through still
damp hair, and he paused, black eyes holding hers
in the glass. 'You seem—strained.'

'Should there be?' She stared back defiantly.
'Should there be something on my mind? Or is that
a guilty conscience needling?'

'Meaning?' he swung round, his mouth tightening

as their glances collided, as Denise tossed scorn across the open space.

'Meaning have you got something to tell me? Something you want to confess. Something linked to Jen, perhaps—and this?' She opened her hand, allowing the scrap of lace to flutter to the floor and, angling her head, held his gaze, the challenge loud in her eyes.

Adam's face darkened, his mouth a thin and angry line. 'You're wrong,' he said simply.

'Am I?' Denise shook her head. 'Oh, no Adam. Not this time. I saw Jen less than a week ago, and that unmistakable fragrance is unique to her. It isn't on general sale yet,' she explained coolly. 'So——' She paused, her eyes flicking over the well-loved body, the lightly tanned physique that created urgent needs she'd rather not acknowledge, and pictures flashed through her mind—Adam and Jen, mouth against mouth, skin against skin. 'So spare me the lies. I know, Adam. I know.'

He shrugged, deliberately offhand, turning back to his reflection, indifference oozing from the pores of his body, and, seeing the free and easy way he combed his hair, Denise felt something snap.

She sprang off the bed, moving quickly to his side. 'Look at me!' she insisted icily. 'Look at me, damn you!' And when Adam didn't move, didn't even glance in her direction, she raised her balled fists, pummelling angrily, uselessly against the taut flesh. 'Look at me,' she repeated, the blows barely registering, and then Adam swung round, anger blazing down from bottomless pools. Snatching at her wrists, he held her fast, iron fingers bruising the delicate skin. 'Adam, you're hurting me,' she protested feebly.

'Am I?' he demanded swiftly. 'Well, in that case, Denise, we're even. You've hurt me. You—Denise Walker— judge, jury and executioner all rolled into one. You've condemned me out of hand and I wouldn't protest my innocence now if my life depended on it.'

'Because you can't,' she threw back swiftly. 'Because we both know the truth. Jen bats her sultry six-inch lashes and the virile Adam Walker can't wait to get her into bed.'

'And what if I did?' he countered coolly. 'It's hardly the end of the world, and how I spend my time is none of your business.'

'Oh, yes, it is!' She snatched back her hands, the sheer force of anger breaking Adam's grip. 'You're married to me,' she spat, eyes wild, nostrils flaring. 'And I refuse to live with a man who's being unfaithful.'

'Are you threatening me?' he asked dangerously. 'Again?' And he shook his head from side to side, the gesture slow and oozing menace. 'You really don't understand, do you, Denise? You just can't follow the rules of the game. Well, let me spell them out for you. I'm answerable to no one. Not to Jen. Not to you. No one. What I do is none of your concern.'

'Wrong, Adam,' she blazed in turn. 'Believe it if

you like, but spare a thought for Kate at least. Think of Kate,' she insisted frigidly. 'Think of the scandal.'

'When you plaster the so-called facts across the billboards?' He laughed, a cold, mirthless sound that grated in her ears. 'You wouldn't dare. And, don't forget, without proof, no one's going to risk upsetting me.'

'Not even the freelance Sadie Graham?' she enquired. And it was her turn to laugh at the expression on his face. 'You see, Adam, it doesn't take much to rustle up a scandalous front page. So——' She paused, eyes frigid, the tilt of her chin aggressive. 'It's up to you. Stay away from Jen or I go now, with never a backward glance.'

'No one gives Adam Walker ultimatums.'

'I do,' she retorted coldly. 'Playing a part I may be, but I won't be taken for a fool. Understand, Adam? As long as you're married to me, you'll conform.'

'Will I?' he challenged. And then he smiled, so, so confident. 'Don't forget,' he pointed out, with a sneering curl of the lips, 'you're under contract—to me. And you can't afford to risk the early termination clause. Jenny,' he cruelly reminded her. 'Cross me and you'll both lose out. And you couldn't risk that, could you, Denise? No!' he sneeringly informed her. 'Not when there's money at stake— Jen's money cushioning a fledgling business.'

Denise dropped her gaze, sealing the truth with her silence. Yet what a waste of time, she derided inwardly. Adam wasn't hers, and Jen was about to reject him. Only Adam, arrogant Adam, didn't have a clue.

The tears came later, when the lights went out and a chilled Denise crept off the balcony and into bed—a bed glaringly empty. Adam could be any-where—the dressing-room, a dozen guest-rooms, or halfway back to Jen in the powerful Alfa Romeo. That was it, then. Over. The sobs rose, Denise doing her best to stifle them. She'd go. First thing tomorrow she'd be on her way. Adam could explain to Kate. Poor Kate, who deserved so much more than life had in store. Could she do that to Kate? Shatter her dreams so cruelly? Denise didn't know. More tears came, suppressed sobs racking her body.

She didn't hear the door, nor the footsteps pad-ding towards her. Just felt the touch, Adam's touch, gentle hands prising her off the sodden pillow, arms folding round and holding her close, rocking, sooth-ing, murmuring words she couldn't hear, didn't need to hear, his lips kissing away the tears, the pain, and a rigid Denise melted in his arms. They were alone and they were together, and nothing in the world intruded—not Kate, not Jen, not the uncertain future. Just Adam. Adam and Denise, eager fingers pushing away the bathrobes; Adam and Denise, arms and legs entwined, mouth kissing mouth, caressing, biting, exciting. Adam and Denise, alone in their world.

'I'm sorry,' Adam murmured as he stretched naked beside her, and he paused, gazing solemnly down by the silvery light of the moon. For a fraction of a second she froze. Sorry. Such a little word, such a convenient word for a range of sins, and then she pushed it away, no longer caring that she was second-best. She loved Adam, and if that meant making do with someone else's crumbs, she hadn't any choice.

She moved, slipping her body into the contours of his, the need to touch and be touched overwhelming, the hiss of indrawn breath as her breasts brushed his chest all the proof she needed that Adam wanted her. The time for words was long since past as hands and mouth created havoc where they touched, the frenzy increasing, the need for satisfaction driving the rest of the world away, and as probing fingers threaded damp curls Denise mewed deep in her throat, arching towards him, her legs parting, Adam sliding into her body, ripples of excitement swelling as the tension mounted, the touch, the taste, the smell, the whole tactile experience so much more than she'd ever known, and she cried out as the release came, Adam's convulsive response triggering wave after wave of shuddering emotion that lifted her and carried her off into a whole new dimension.

'Friends again?' he asked a lifetime later.

Denise nodded, smiling happily up into Adam's probing eyes. 'Friends again,' she told him softly, and then the imp inside gained the upper hand. 'Until next time.'

Adam laughed, pulling her towards him, his beautiful naked body already primed for more, exploring hands caressing her tingling skin. 'What I like about the rows,' he told her confidentially, 'is being allowed to show how much I'm sorry—actions speaking louder than words, I hope.'

'Hush,' she told him throatily, swollen lips brushing his mouth and proving the point with simple eloquence. He laughed again, but didn't reply. He didn't need to. Every touch, every kiss, each and every sultry glance spoke volumes.

CHAPTER NINE

'I DON'T want to go.'

'What do you mean, you don't want to go? I'm this year's host, Denise. I can hardly arrive by myself. If I go, my wife goes. Simple.'

Not to me, she felt like retorting. Only she didn't, biting back an acid reply. His wife. Oh, yes. If the final check-up allowed it Kate was leaving at the end of the week, and unless Denise was pregnant her role as Adam's wife would then be at an end.

'I—I think I should stay with Kate,' she explained. 'She's looking pale, and though she wouldn't dream of asking——'

'Exactly. Kate won't fuss. Maria will be here in any case. Now, will you please hurry and pack an overnight bag? I need to be in London by three.' He turned away, clearly expecting no refusal, sorting through some papers in the briefcase on the bed.

Denise didn't move, simply stood and watched, grey eyes full of mute appeal.

The faint rustle ceased as Adam glanced up. 'Well?' he queried, black eyes impatient. 'Now what's the problem? Nothing to wear? Need a new dress? If we make a move now, you can drop in at Claud's and pick yourself out a whole new creation.'

'I bought a new dress last week,' she needled. Or

153

rather, Adam did. He'd flown to Paris on business and had arrived home with the most exquisite froth of silk and lace Denise had ever seen. She should have been thrilled, but wasn't, aware of the reason—her first public appearance as Adam's wife, the Press Barons' Charity Ball. And at the back of her mind the storm clouds were gathering. Jen. Denise couldn't be sure, but she had the awful suspicion that her publicity-hungry cousin would be there—flaunting Zak and that enormous sapphire and diamond ring.

'So?' Adam shrugged. 'One dress, two, a dozen. I can afford it.'

'Oh, I'm sure you can,' she retorted sharply. 'And if you choose to waste it, that's up to you. But I'll spend my money my way.'

'Please yourself. But it's one of the perks of the job. If the money's there, why not use it?'

'Because the "job", as you quaintly call it, will soon be over.'

'Meaning?' He straightened then, his six-foot-three-inch form towering above her, and, watching him, Denise felt her heart skip a beat. She loved him. Oh, how she loved him. And there was nothing she could do to cushion the blow Jen was about to deal.

'Meaning just that. When Kate leaves, I leave. End of contract, remember?'

'Ah, yes. I suppose you're right,' he acknowledged drily. 'But only a rat would expect you to pack up and leave while the plane's taxiing for take-off. Take your time, Denise, take as long as you like. But if parts of the job were a drag,' he slipped in slyly, 'you should have said. I'd have been happy to renegotiate your duties.'

Denise went white. 'Don't be so revolting,' she snapped. 'That isn't what I meant, and well you know it.'

'Do I?' He shrugged. 'I thought—hoped—that you wouldn't find me wanting——'

'No! You're a man of the world. And even prissy little me could recognise an expert.'

'My, my, the kitten has claws.' And though the words were mocking, his mouth was taut. 'What's the matter? Beginning to realise what you'll be missing?'

'Not at all,' she told him crisply. 'It might be a blow to your ego, Adam, but if and when I need a man, I'll not be short of choice. They're ten a penny,' she told him pithily. 'And cheap at twice the price.'

'You've changed your tune,' he derided in turn, a dull flush darkening his features. 'What happened to the sweet and innocent Denise who was saving herself for love?'

'She grew up, Adam, the hard way,' she retorted, but deep inside the taunt had reached its barb. Oh, Jen. Did you have to mock? Did you have to laugh at me with Adam? And the thought of Adam's scorn was almost the last straw.

'So I discovered,' he observed lazily. 'Luckily for me.'

'Luck didn't come into it. You couldn't find Jen, so you took the next best thing.'

'Oh, I don't know.' His eyes narrowed as he mulled the charge over. 'You and Jen are—different.'

'As chalk and cheese. Town-mouse and country-cousin. And the high-powered Mr Walker knows which one he prefers.'

'He certainly does,' he agreed, with an unexpected flash of humour.

Denise saw red. 'She isn't worth it, Adam,' she heatedly declared. 'Jen may be everything a man could want but she's as shallow as a lake in a desert. She's my only living relative and I love her dearly, but that doesn't blind me to her faults. She'll hurt you. She's done it already. She'll do it again.'

'And do you care?'

'Yes, I care. You're a man—oh, ruthless in business, I know, but there's another side, the caring, loving side. I've seen you with Kate. And as for Jen—' She stopped, swallowed, shrugged, suddenly afraid to say too much. 'Jen did let you down.'

'Only once,' he told her simply. 'Only once. And not even Jen would risk it twice. Not to me, I promise.'

Denise closed her eyes. He wasn't listening. He didn't want to hear and she could only hope and pray that Jen had the sense not to cross him. Not yet, at least, and certainly not in public. It would be the one thing Adam could never forgive, and though Zak Peters had influence, Adam Walker plc was in a different league. And then she shrugged. If Adam and Jen chose to self-destruct, that was up to them.

With Adam tied up with business, Denise went shopping. Nothing major, just underwear and tights for the dress she'd be wearing—stunning silver with layers and layers of net in a very full skirt. When she'd first tried it on her cheeks had flamed, the tiny bodice seeming indecent and staying in place heaven alone knew how. But Adam had bought it. Whatever the reason, the dress had been a gift from the man she loved, and so Denise would wear it.

Back at the hotel, she climbed into the bath, needing a long, hot soak to soothe taut nerves. It didn't help. Nothing would, she decided and, steeling herself for the worst, reached for the phone. A waste of time, she was willing to bet, but she would try. She got the answerphone. After twenty minutes and a dozen wasted calls, Denise gave up. *If* Jen was in England, she wasn't at any of her usual haunts, and a glimmer of hope was born. Maybe, just maybe, Denise was fretting over nothing.

'You look—simply stunning.'

Denise lost her step as the heated glance sent her pulse-rate soaring, smouldering eyes locking with hers as Adam led the way on to the floor.

'Thank you,' she murmured tightly, cheeks tinged with red. Not that she believed him. The easy words, like the traditional opening dance, were just another social chore, and with the world's most beautiful women watching from the sidelines she'd have to be a fool not to know.

'Try to relax,' Adam entreated, sensing her unease. 'In another five minutes the floor will be packed and you can lose yourself in the crowd.'

'It's the crowd that worries me,' she wryly explained. 'The pushing, shoving, menacing crowd, with their cameras and flashbulbs. Heaven knows how they earned the name *gentlemen* of the Press.'

'Hmm.' His eyes narrowed suddenly, and he pulled Denise close as he swung her round. 'And not all gentlemen either,' he murmured, 'unless my eyes deceive me.'

She followed the line of his gaze, her heart skipping a beat as she recognised the familiar mocking smile. How did she get in? Denise wondered sickly, since Press badges were rationed and Adam had vetted them all. And then it hit her. Sadie Graham had come as a guest.

'Not by my leave,' Adam confirmed, and as the music changed and the dance-floor filled he added grimly, 'Still, that's no problem. I'll get rid of her.'

'No.' Denise pulled up sharp. 'Don't make a scene. Please, Adam. The woman's here. She must have been invited. Don't give her ammunition for tomorrow's sleazy tabloids. Let her stay. Ignore her. Please.'

It was a never-ending moment, Adam tense and visibly angry, Denise afraid and not sure why. She gazed up at him, grey eyes silently pleading, instinct telling her that the woman was trouble and that if

Adam moved now, Sadie Graham would release her poison, would spoil the evening before it began. And she was already so afraid that the night was heading for disaster.

Then Adam smiled, banishing the tension. Dipping his head, he brushed his lips against hers. 'Come on,' he murmured easily. 'Let's grab ourselves a drink. You're right, of course. Much better to ignore her.'

It wasn't easy, the woman seeming to stick like glue to Adam and Denise. The buffet, the bars, the dance-floor—wherever they went, Sadie Graham was close behind. And since Adam quickly developed the knack of looking straight through her, Denise was left to do the same.

When Sadie Graham unexpectedly disappeared, Denise seized the chance to slip to the Ladies. Eleven o'clock. If Jen was set on making an entrance, it would have to be soon, and with Adam's speech and the toasts scheduled for midnight, the next sixty minutes would be crucial. Denise brushed her hair, critical eyes checking her make-up. She'd do, she decided wryly, and with a mental shrug of resignation, turned and headed out. It came as no surprise to find that she wasn't alone. Sadie Graham lounged against the door.

'Get out of my way,' Denise almost spat, her eyes needles of ice.

'Why?' the older woman stalled. 'What gives you the right to order me around?'

'If I was giving orders,' Denise informed her

coolly, 'you wouldn't still be here. In fact, you wouldn't have been admitted in the first place.'

'Wouldn't I? Well, well, well. Who'd have thought it? Adam Walker's mouse of a wife has spirit.'

'Don't tell me you hadn't noticed,' Denise derided sweetly. 'After weeks and weeks of tailing me, I'm surprised there's anything left to discover.'

'And what makes you think I'm following you around?'

'Just an impression,' Denise admitted airily. 'Like the proverbial bad penny, you turn up with monotonous regularity.'

The other woman shrugged. 'Maybe you're right,' she agreed almost pleasantly. 'But don't flatter yourself, my dear. If I was gathering copy I wouldn't waste a word on you.'

'Good. Let's hope you keep it that way.' She made to sweep past, brought up sharp by a calculated side-step.

'Not so fast,' Sadie almost crooned. 'I haven't finished with you yet.'

'And me so boring, so mousy, such an unimportant nobody?' Denise drawled. 'What can the lady mean?'

Green eyes narrowed dangerously. '*You know*,' she insisted gleefully. 'And if you don't, you're a bigger fool than I took you for.' She glanced at her watch, a strange smile playing about the corners of her mouth. 'And in another half-hour all the world will know, won't they, Denise?'

'I don't know what you're talking about,' Denise

retorted calmly, a lot more calmly than she felt. Her insides were churning, a horrible premonition taking hold. This venomous woman knew. Adam, Denise, Jen—the entire sorry tangle. Sadie Graham had scented a story, and Denise could almost see the headlines: '*Ménage à Trois* Stales', perhaps, or 'Adam Walker's Family Affair is Over'. And, since Kate rarely read the English papers, it would be Adam who'd be hurt. Adam—hard as nails on the outside, but vulnerable where Jen was concerned. Vulnerable, in love—and about to be cruelly and publicly rejected.

'Don't you, Denise?' Sadie Graham smiled again. 'Well, don't let me spoil the surprise.'

Adam rose to greet her as Denise reached their table, sharp eyes logging the strain. 'Is something wrong?' he demanded swiftly. 'Has something happened? Has that woman been pestering you?'

Denise shook her head, gazing up into Adam's solemn face. 'No,' she lied, crossing her fingers and forcing a smile. 'Everything's fine.' Everything's fine—for now. But the time bomb was ticking away the last few minutes of peace.

'Ladies and gentlemen.' The drum roll, the introduction, Adam's appearance on the dais. Denise was left alone, alone in a crowd, champagne-flute clutched in rigid fingers. Her eyes swept the room, looking for Jen, the spotlights dazzling, heads and faces nothing but a blur. She gulped the icy liquid, reaching for another. It had come. The moment she'd been dreading. Adam was making his speech, the whole room attentive, held in the palm of his hand, his easy words raising smiles. Then it was almost over; Denise was attuned to the cues—the thanks, the money raised, the children who would benefit. And then—the unexpected commotion.

Denise closed her eyes as the spotlight switched, cameras flashing in the doorway. A lone reporter broke away from the crowd, jostling Jen and her escort, dashing across the dance-floor, and raised his voice to Adam, who'd paused, mouth set tight.

'Mr Walker, have you anything to say about Miss Elliot's shock engagement?'

And then the mob moved, sensing blood.

'Mr Walker, is it true your marriage is a sham. . .?'

'That your so-called wife was her cousin's stand-in. . .?'

'That the pay-off will be in millions. . .?'

'That you tried—unsuccessfully—to buy off your rival. . .?'

The questions went on and on, camera bulbs flashing, Adam's face masking the surprise, the pain, his eyes crossing the sea of heads and locking with Jen's. And Denise could only watch, thankful that the mob had forgotten her existence, the pain growing as Adam's hurt became hers and she forced herself to face the awful truth at last. Adam loved Jen, would always love Jen, and her own tenuous place in his life was over.

And then he turned his head, eyes seeking hers, a compelling gaze on rigid features.

He raised his hands, the noise quelling in an

instant, and the whole room held its breath as Adam prolonged the suspense. Reaching for a glass from the table, he raised it to his lips. 'Ladies and gentlemen,' he murmured easily, 'another toast. To my cousin-in-law and her lucky fiancé. And to my wife—who means more to me than words can possibly convey. To Jen—and Denise.'

To Jen and Denise. The names echoed round the room, the camera bulbs flashing, the music blaring, the awkward moment over. And Denise, seeing Adam smile as he wove his way towards her, watching as he paused to talk, paused to laugh, suddenly couldn't take any more. She had to escape. She had to get away.

She halted in the foyer. They'd arrived by car so she'd need to take a taxi—if she could find one. Time. She hadn't time to stand and wait. Adam would come and find her. And she had to get away, had to get away. She set off on foot, the flimsy high heels an unforeseen hindrance and she kicked them off, cursing lightly under her breath. She bent to pick them up before setting off again, hitching up her dress, oblivious of the stares she raised in people passing by, oblivious of the cold, hard pavement beneath her feet. Almost there. The Walker World. Adam's hotel. A thin drizzle of rain went unheeded. Almost there. And yet, she acknowledged painfully, Adam was sure to be close behind. She choked back the pain, choked back the tears. But of course, she castigated herself harshly. Why come looking for

Denise except to show the world he loved her—a public display to salvage his pride?

She burst into the foyer, cold, wet and dishevelled, but the girl behind the desk was too well-trained to betray her surprise.

'Mr Walker rang,' she explained as Denise snatched her key.

'I'll bet,' Denise derided, but she didn't wait for the words. Adam had nothing to say that she could possibly want to hear, and she ignored the lift, taking the stairs, thankful that the hour was late and there was no one to see her. Her suite. Their suite. Their bed. Their life together—over.

She stepped out of the dress, leaving it on the floor, a sodden heap of silk and lace, as she raided the wardrobes for something to wear, something she had bought. She would go, and she'd take nothing that Adam had paid for. She'd take nothing. She wanted nothing from Adam, nothing at all. Except the one thing she'd never be entitled to. His love. She almost snorted with derision. Adam's love was already given—to Jen. She grabbed her coat and handbag and headed for the door—careering head-first into Adam's restraining arms.

'Hey, not so fast,' he murmured easily.

'Let go of me,' Denise demanded, squirming at his touch.

'All in good time,' he soothed. 'But it's late. you're cold and drenched by the look of things, and you and I need to talk.'

'Oh, no!' Denise was scathing. 'We're over,

Adam. This fiasco has gone far enough. It's over. I quit, as of now.'

'Oh, no, you don't,' he informed her tightly. 'You're married to me, you're working for me, and no one makes my decisions for me.'

'Jen did,' she reminded cruelly.

His mouth tightened, black eyes pools of hate. 'Leave Jen out of this.'

'Why?' Denise demanded. 'Isn't Jen the reason we're here, the reason you've followed so quickly? Jen lets you down, smacks your face in public, and hey presto, Adam Walker suddenly needs a wife. To salvage his pride. Well, the rest of the world might be fooled but don't expect me to swallow it.'

'I was telling them the truth.'

'The truth? Hah! "My wife",' she cruelly mocked, '"who means more to me than words can possibly convey." I know, Adam,' she told him frigidly. 'I know what you said, I know what you mean. I've been useful. I've fooled Kate, deceived her—deceived a sick old lady. How proud do you think that makes me, Adam? How proud does it make you? Because it makes me feel sordid.' And she swung away, crossing to the windows, the necklace of lights along the Embankment blurring before her eyes.

He moved in behind her, his presence unmistakable, Denise shockingly attuned to his unique maleness. She folded her arms, suddenly chilled, the need to feel his arms around her, comforting, holding, protecting, an overwhelming urge she had to fight. She needed Adam, but Adam didn't need her—except as a sop, a decoy, a temporary arrangement to fool the world and deceive a sick old lady.

'Denise?'

'Don't touch me,' she spat, shaking off the hand that reached for her shoulder. 'Don't you *ever* touch me again.'

'Why?' he demanded, suddenly angry. 'Why, Denise, why?' And he spun her round to face him as Denise visibly cringed.

'I'm warning you, Adam, lay a finger on me and you'll wish you'd never been born. Sadie Graham makes a useful contact.'

'You wouldn't dare.'

'Wouldn't I?'

There was a pause, the atmosphere so thick she could have cut it with a knife. And then Adam swung away, crossing to the mini-bar and pouring himself a brandy.

'Make mine a vodka,' she rasped, the memory scything through. A dash of tonic, a slice of lemon and lots and lots of ice. Only she didn't say the words and didn't need the ice. She was frozen already, deep inside.

Adam's lips twisted as he handed her the glass. 'Here's to old times,' he toasted bitterly. 'And to the future, whatever it may bring.'

'We haven't got a future,' she told him witheringly. 'Leastways, not together.'

'But we could have, Denise. Don't you see?' he entreated urgently. 'We could have.'

'Oh, yes?' she derided, the rawness of the pain causing her to sneer. 'And what the hell do you take me for? It might suit you having a woman to keep your bed warm, but I want more from life than a tumble between the sheets and a wardrobe full of clothes.'

'Then tell me what you want.'

'So you can go out and buy it? Oh, Adam,' she mocked, her cool grey eyes raking the lines of his face. 'Even your countless millions can't work miracles.'

'Maybe not,' he acknowledged. 'But money helps. It cushions, it opens lots of doors. And we could have a life together—if that's what you want.'

'Well, I don't.' She swung away, hating the pain that was etched in the angles of his face. Adam loved Jen, and Denise knew how much he was hurting. But if Adam could live with second best, Denise couldn't. She loved Adam, and if she couldn't have his love, she wouldn't make do with the crumbs on offer. She had her pride. It was all— or nothing. And she wasn't about to kid herself on that.

'So—you're determined to go?'

'Yes,' she told him, tilting her chin in defiance. 'I'm going now.'

'Oh, no!' He smiled grimly as he threw himself down in a chair, impatient fingers tugging at the bow tie, snapping the buttons of the dress-shirt, the casual result unexpectedly appealing.

Could she stay? she asked herself, weakening,

wavering. Could she live with Adam, day in and day out, knowing he didn't love her, knowing there'd be long nights alone while Adam took his pleasure elsewhere? Could she live with the pain, with the easy deception? No! No! No! And then Adam's words sank in. 'What did you say?' she enquired politely, angling her head.

'I said no, you can't leave now. I simply won't let you.'

'Well, have I got news for you,' she retorted, heading for the door.

He let her go, and she was absurdly, illogically disappointed, and then she reached the foyer to find the exit barred and the doorman conspicuously absent. She spun round, but the night-desk too was glaringly unstaffed.

She reached the fire door as common sense returned. She couldn't. She'd escape, sure enough, but she'd leave chaos in her wake. A couple of hundred guests roused by the fire-bell, and worse, emergency vehicles rushing to the scene, putting other lives at risk. 'OK, Adam,' she murmured acidly. 'You win—again. But you'd better make it the last time.'

'Enjoy your walk?' he enquired as she strolled back in. He hadn't moved except to remove his jacket, which he'd draped across a chair.

'It was—short, sharp and sobering,' she told him coolly. 'It's getting to be a habit, Adam, this medieval practice of locking up your women. Pity you didn't do the same with Jen.'

'Jen's over and done with,' he told her sharply.

'So I gathered,' she replied. And then she walked slowly, deliberately across the sea of carpet. 'I'm going to bed,' she announced calmly over her shoulder. 'Alone. And just to make sure it stays that way, I'll be locking the door. But that won't be a problem, will it, Adam?' she pointedly reminded him. 'You own the place; you can have your pick of rooms. And if by any chance you're feeling lonely, a word of advice: spend some money. It shouldn't take much to rustle up a consolation prize.'

'I want you,' he said simply, stopping her dead in her tracks.

She spun round, grey eyes spitting scorn. 'Me?' She laughed, a cold, harsh sound that echoed horribly inside her head. 'No, Adam,' she contradicted in a voice devoid of emotion. 'Be honest. You've never wanted me. But with Jen denting your pride in public, you're snatching at the next best thing. Only I won't let you. Not any more. So when Kate flies out, I walk out as well—for good.'

CHAPTER TEN

'YOU'RE not happy, are you, my dear?'

Denise glanced up, colour flooding her face before draining away, leaving her cheeks as pale as chalk. She swallowed hard, seeing the love and concern in Kate's expression. So many lies, she realised, racking her brains for something to say, something trite and meaningless to soothe Kate's fears. And with just twenty-four hours till Kate flew home surely she could manage to keep up the pretence? And then she read the message in the older woman's eyes.

'You know, don't you?' she asked.

'About Adam and your cousin?' Kate nodded. 'I've known all along,' she told her simply. 'Jenny Elliot, the up-and-coming model whose name was linked with my grandson's. Oh, yes.' Kate smiled wryly. 'I may not read the papers but I've never been short of friends, and when the engagement was announced I was quickly informed.'

'But—I don't understand.' Denise was bewildered. 'Why didn't you say? You must have known there was something wrong.'

'Or something right,' Kate replied enigmatically. 'Don't you see? It would have been easy enough for Adam to explain your cousin's absence. Only he

170

didn't, he turned up with you. The question is, why?'

'He wanted to make you happy,' Denise said simply.

'I suppose he did,' Kate agreed, smiling. 'But it was more than that. Adam was stinging. Jen had hurt his pride and you helped give it back to him.'

'But everyone knew the engagement was a sham.'

'Everyone except me, in theory. But deep down inside, I still think there was something else—another reason, a simple reason.'

Denise shrugged. Kate was wrong. The explanation was plain. Kate had been dying and Adam had been determined to make her last months happy. Only Kate had been given the gift of life. Test results had shown what no one had expected. The pioneering laser treatment had eased the pressure on her brain and Kate had a normal life ahead of her now. No worries, no hospitals, no sterile months in a clinic. And Denise was free—Adam's final hold was broken. Oh, yes, she hadn't kidded herself on that one. Jen's shock announcement might have set the ball in motion, but as long as the truth was kept from Kate, Denise would never have been free. The relief was overwhelming, yet the pain didn't seem to ease.

'I'm sorry,' Denise said simply, knowing Kate would understand and would forgive.

'No.' Kate shook her head. '*I'm* sorry. Sorry it didn't work out the way I hoped. I didn't know your cousin, but I'd heard enough about her, and when

Adam turned up with you, it was the answer to my prayers. And you loved Adam, loved him enough to cover for your cousin's careless behaviour. You loved Adam, and a meddlesome old woman who should have known better decided to play God. It was unforgivable,' she explained, with another tight smile. 'And if pushing you into marriage was bad enough, hinting about a baby was little short of blackmail. I thought——'

'That a baby would keep us together? No.' Denise shook her head, the tears dangerously close. 'The baby would have been for you, Adam's gift of love for you.' But that was all, she admitted as the hurt grew. Everything Adam had done had been for Kate.

She went home, the memories crowding in—Jen and Denise growing up, squabbling like sisters, Jen and Adam, Adam and Denise—and long, solitary weeks passed, with Adam's letters destroyed unread and the answerphone screening the messages. It was no good. She had to get away, needed time to think, and when an old school-friend offered her a lifeline, Denise seized the chance to escape. For along with the pain had come the nausea. And suspicion. And the truth. She was pregnant. She was carrying Adam's child and she was alone—never so alone.

The sound of footsteps roused her, the tap, tap, tap of stiletto heels, and Denise glanced up in alarm. It was warm in the garden and she must have dozed

off, the book she'd been reading lying closed on her
lap. The sound grew louder, and still she didn't
move. Visitors? Her lips twisted wryly. Hardly. No
one knew where to find her, and she sat perfectly
still, listening, waiting. A familiar figure rounded
the corner.

'Found you!'

'Jen!' Denise was off the bench in an instant, her
reactions instinctive as she flung herself into her
cousin's outstretched arms. 'What on earth are you
doing here?'

'Would you believe, looking for you?' Jen smiled
brightly. 'I'm getting married,' she explained, sitting
gingerly down on the plain wooden bench and
wrinkling her nose in distaste.

'Zak?' Denise enquired politely, for an awful
moment thinking of Adam.

'Of course. Don't sound so surprised. I was bound
to fall in love sooner or later. And talking of love,
what happened to you and Adam?'

Denise shrugged, flushing painfully under her
cousin's candid gaze. 'You did,' she told her frankly.
'Adam wanted you. And I couldn't bear the thought
of being second-best.'

'But we were over months ago,' Jen declared, a
tiny frown creasing her features. 'I thought I'd made
it plain. Once Adam married you, he and I were
through.'

'But you wanted Adam. You *said* you wanted
Adam.'

'Maybe I did—once,' Jen agreed offhandedly.

'But then I met Zak. He taught me what I'd been missing.'

Maybe, Denise silently acknowledged. But it hadn't stopped Jen playing games, hadn't stopped Adam crawling back. And though Jen felt sure of her future now, how long before the rot set in—the boredom, the need for something new? And with Adam waiting in the wings, Jen would never be short of fun.

'So?' Jen prompted, wide eyes fastened on Denise.

'So——' Denise shrugged. She'd nothing to say. Not about Adam. And then the anger surged, catching her off-guard. 'Why, Jen?' she demanded heatedly. 'Why did you do it? You had everything—money, fame, Zak. You had everything you could possibly need and yet you couldn't leave me Adam. Why, Jen, why?'

'I don't know what you're talking about. I haven't seen Adam for months.'

'Don't lie!' Denise entreated frigidly. 'Don't pretend. You wanted revenge. Adam let you down and you had to hit back at someone. Only not Adam. Oh, no. You didn't choose Adam, you chose me. Me! How could you, Jen? How could you?'

'Look, Denise, if you'd tell me what you're talking about——'

'You know. Don't pretend you don't.' Denise sprang up, crossing the lawn to the stream—the miniature River Windrush—that meandered through the garden. It was a slice of paradise, the isolated cottage in the Cotswolds where Denise had gone to ground, only now she'd been found and her precious peace was shattered, plunging her back into the realities of life. Life without Adam.

She heard a rustle at her side, the distinctive whiff of musk triggering a host of memories, but Denise didn't speak, swallowing the pain along with the anger. Jen was—just Jen. Self-centred, spoiled, thoughtless. And, in a way, she'd done Denise a favour, made her face the truth. Adam didn't love her but, gentleman to the end, he'd want to take care of his child. And then *he'd* be trapped. Denise would have trapped him. And sooner or later he'd grow to resent her. Resentment, indifference, hate. At the end of it all, the hate. So—she didn't have a choice. She'd make a new life for herself and the baby.

'Was it the ball?' Jen asked, placing a tentative hand on her arm.

Denise shook her head. 'No,' she said simply. 'It wasn't the ball.'

Jen sighed heavily. 'Then it was the handkerchief. I should have known. Oh, Denise, I'm sorry.' And then, in the softest of voices, 'Would you let me explain? Please, Denise, I need to explain.'

'So you can salve your conscience?'

Their eyes locked, one pair full of pain, the other heavy with compassion.

'It didn't happen,' Jen said simply. 'However it looked, nothing happened.'

'Not for the want of trying,' Denise accused

bitterly. 'Don't you see, even if it were true, Adam wants you. He's always wanted you. I was—just convenient.' And she shook herself free of Jen's restraining hand, crouching, placing her fingers in the ice-cold river, allowing the water to numb her flesh, wishing she could do the same for the pain inside her heart.

'He laughed at me,' Jen explained, as if she hadn't heard. 'We met by chance in the hotel bar, and when Adam walked me to my room I talked him into coming in. Adam wanted me, I was so sure he wanted me, and I was going to make him pay for making me look a fool, for marrying you. Only he turned me down. Do you know how much that hurt?' she cried with unexpected vehemence. 'Have you any idea of the pain it caused? To know that my mousy little cousin could keep Adam Walker faithful.'

'Faithful? To me?' Denise almost laughed. 'Oh, Jen, you really must be joking.'

'Must I?' Jen shook her head. 'That's what I couldn't accept. That Adam had finally found what he'd been looking for. You. Only I didn't want to believe it, kidded nyself that he was hitting back at me. And I wanted my revenge. When Adam reached the point of no return, I was going to throw it back in his face. But he laughed at me. Me!' she said again bitterly. 'He turned me down flat and then he laughed. Don't you see?' she entreated, dropping to her knees, oblivious of the grass-stains on the horrendously expensive skirt. 'He didn't want me any more. He didn't want me, didn't need me, didn't love me. Because he had you. Adam loves you.'

'Don't be ridiculous,' Denise derided. 'Haven't you done enough without rubbing salt in? Adam married me because——'

'Because he loved you,' Jen cut in. 'And, believe me, only a fool would doubt it. That night at the ball Adam told me, told the world, told *you*, that he loved you.'

'And the handkerchief.'

'Was a plant. Cruel of me, I know, but I wasn't thinking. I wanted to hurt—you more than Adam—and for once in my life I really do feel ashamed.' She sighed heavily. 'And now it's too late to turn back the clock.' She dropped her head, defeat written into the lines of her body, and, watching her, Denise felt the ice begin to melt. Jen was telling the truth. Her beautiful, elegant cousin was giving her the truth.

'Jen,' she acknowledged in the strangest of voices, 'I love you. Heaven knows why, but I still love you. But if you ever, ever, ever again come between me and Adam, then I promise you, Jen, next time you'll get more than just a ducking.' And she reached out, hands connecting briefly at the shoulder, connecting and pushing, a startled Jen losing her balance, wild fingers clutching at the air, the exquisite face white with shock as she reached the point of no return. She seemed to hang in space, a moment frozen in time, and then she slumped, toppling slowly, awkwardly into the water.

'Next time, Jen,' Denise told her spluttering, outraged cousin, 'next time I'll half drown you.'

'Adam?'

He glanced up, a range of expressions crossing his face, surprise, delight, uncertainty battling for control. And then the shutters came down, just Adam's black eyes politely returning her gaze.

'You've come for your things,' he stated flatly. 'Sorry, Denise. I know I promised to send them on, but——' He shrugged, standing up and crossing to the window.

'How's Kate?' Denise enquired when he made no effort to speak.

'Fit as a fiddle and off on her travels, determined to see the world. She said to send her love when you did get back in touch. *When*,' he added bitterly, turning his head and pinning her with the intensity of his gaze. 'Not if. She'd more belief than I had. Except—you've only come for your things.'

'Maybe,' Denise said softly, so softly the word was almost a caress.

'Don't play games,' he entreated frigidly. 'You're Denise Elliot, not Jen. If you've something to say, then say it. I'm not in the mood for charades.'

'I'm Denise *Walker*,' she pointed out, her heart thumping painfully. He was hurting inside and she could feel the pain, yet still she wasn't sure. Was it Jen he loved? Or was it her?

'Ah, yes. Denise Walker. Mrs Adam Walker. My wife. *My wife.*' And he laughed, a cold, empty sound that rent the air. 'You could have saved yourself a journey, Denise. A phone call. A letter. A terse request for your things and I'd have happily obeyed. But then I might have sent the things I'd bought, and you couldn't risk that, could you, my love? No,' he told her bitterly, 'heaven forbid you'd want reminders of me. See Maria,' he entreated coldly. 'If you tell her what you want, I'm sure she'll lend a hand.'

'If you want me to I'll go,' she said softly. She had to know, had to be sure, had to hear the words from Adam. If he wanted her, he had to say the words. And if he didn't. . .

'Yes, woman,' he retorted harshly. 'Go! Get out of my sight. Get out of my life,' he added cruelly, half under his breath, and the tears welled up, scalding tears that hovered on her lashes.

She turned away. Adam was right. She shouldn't have come, shouldn't have opened the wounds. Denise reminded him of Jen. Jen. A picture flashed through her mind—her fastidious cousin kneeling at the riverside, stiletto heels dusty, wood and grass-stains on her skirt. Jen, who'd taken the trouble to track her down, blue eyes silently pleading. She'd given her the truth and Denise was a fool for doubting it. And if Denise had her pride, Adam was filled with it. He'd been hurt. He'd told the world that he loved Denise and she'd thrown it back in his face. So—— She licked her dry lips. It was up to her.

She spun round. 'Fine,' she told him briskly. 'If that's what you want. And what Adam Walker wants, Adam Walker gets, hey, Adam?'

'If you say so,' he replied, seemingly indifferent, going back to the window.

'I do,' she countered pertly. 'And since your wish is my every command, I'll go. But before I do you'll listen, and you'd better listen well, because I'll only say this once. I was wrong, Adam, about a lot of things, but I never doubted the way I feel about you. I love you, Adam. I've always loved you.' There was a long, long pause, Adam's stiff back cruelly unrelenting, not a flicker, not a thread of interest, and she twisted away, heading for the door, the tears coursing silently, scaldingly down her cheeks. She reached the steps as Adam's voice sliced across the room.

'Hold it right there!' he commanded.

'Why?' she countered, stopping dead, the elation surging. 'Why should I do what you ask? Ah, yes,' she added swiftly, 'I'd almost forgotten. What Adam Walker wants, Adam Walker gets.'

'Not always,' he replied, moving in behind, close enough to touch yet continuing to deny her. 'Not where you're concerned, Denise. You're a much too stubborn lady and I love you to distraction. But if you could, just this once, do as I ask, I'd be very grateful,' And then, when Denise didn't reply, didn't move, didn't seem to draw breath despite the electricity crackling between them, he added softly, pleadingly, 'Tell me, Denise. Tell me again that you love me.'

She spun round, her smile radiant, eyes brimming with tears—tears of happiness. 'Oh, Adam,' she murmured, a wealth of love in the simple words.

He didn't wait to hear the rest, gathering her to him, almost squeezing the breath from her body as he swung her round and round. 'Denise, Denise, Denise, I love you. I love you, woman,' he murmured huskily, and then his mouth claimed hers, urgently, frenetically, the pressure easing as the kiss went on, as Adam felt the trembles ripple through her body. 'I love you,' he said again simply. 'And you'll never know how good it feels just to say the words.'

'Oh, yes, I will,' she contradicted smokily, the eyes holding his smouldering with promise.

He swept her up, striding easily across to the enormous leather sofa.

'Adam!' she protested feebly as he placed her among the cushions, urgent fingers beginning to undress her. 'What about Maria?'

'Hush, woman,' he commanded, with a tender, lazy smile. 'We're alone. Just you and me. And I'm going to make love to my wife wherever the fancy takes me. And with a dozen rooms to choose from, it could be a busy afternoon. And evening,' he added between kisses. 'And tomorrow, my love, we'll be able to start all over again.'

He kissed her, starting with her mouth, his lips moving down, following the trail that his hands had blazed. Skirt, blouse, panties, bra—sure fingers disposed of her clothes as a branding mouth caressed her glowing skin.

'You're the most beautiful woman in the world,' he told her solemnly when Denise lay naked on the cushions. 'And I never thought I'd see you again, not like this. And believe me, my love, simply looking is an honour.'

'My turn now,' she told him smokily, kneeling and cradling his face in her hands. She kissed him briefly, searingly briefly. 'I love you,' she murmured, lips gliding across the stubble on his chin and revelling in the texture. 'I love you, Adam.' And her mouth moved down as her fingers snapped open the buttons on his shirt, exploring fingers raking the mass of hair across the powerful chest, thumbs brushing his nipples. Adam trembled beneath her touch, groaning as she dipped her head, swirling her tongue across the straining tips, and Denise smiled inside as she urged this tiger of a man back against the cushions. 'Not yet,' she whispered throatily. 'Not yet.'

And when Adam lay quite naked, his lightly tanned body gleaming in the afternoon glow, Denise smiled, lights dancing in her eyes as she hungrily devoured each and every straining line of him.

'Oh, Adam,' she murmured wondrously. 'You're so beautiful, and I want you. I want you so badly that it hurts.'

He moved swiftly, catching her to him, the hug brief and reassuring as he changed their positions,

Denise now writhing beneath him as hands and fingers explored her body, branding where they roamed. Words, Adam's words, magic words poured over her, soothing and exciting, soothing and inflaming. Greedy lips nuzzled her straining nipples, sucking, biting, the pain exquisite, desire flooding her body, an aching need that Adam refused to satisfy, every touch, every taste, every smouldering glance fanning the flames, stoking the fires.

'Adam, Adam, Adam,' she cried in anguish, and still he denied her, his mouth moving down, exploring the valley between her breasts—tongue, lips, fingers playing havoc with her body, creating havoc in her mind, creating heaven on earth. And then, as urgent fingers found her moist and ready, as the shudders began, as the waves of heat began to convulse her, 'Please, Adam, please.'

His answer was a laugh, a throaty chuckle that filled her with delight, and then he was inside her, the contours of his body moulded perfectly to hers, the tension spiralling out of control as Adam cried out in bitter-sweet anguish, carrying Denise away on the whirling, swirling breakers of pure and unashamed pleasure. . .

'And that, madam,' he told her later, much, much later, 'is the last time you walk out on me. Understand?'

'Yes, sir!' she teasingly retorted, nestling snugly against him. They lay on the sofa, arms and legs entwined, the afternoon sun beginning to dip in the sky. And she was happy, deliriously happy.

'Adam?' she murmured thoughtfully, her fingers caressing his rippling skin.

'Mmm, my love?' he lazily replied, lips nuzzling the column of her neck, nuzzling and nipping.

'Why didn't you tell me? Why didn't you explain? I thought you loved Jen——'

'Love Jen? Oh, no! After Celeste I didn't think I'd ever fall in love again. I couldn't risk the pain. And then it hit me. You stood there, eyes spitting fire, the lines of your body shooting hate and anger, and I was lost. And I didn't know what to do to attract your attention. And then I found the lever I needed to hold you——'

'Ah, yes, the money. Jen's golden eggs——'

'No, my love,' he murmured in anguish. 'Never that. I may have said the words, but deep inside I never believed them. Instead I used Kate——'

'Kate! Oh, Adam, wait till we tell Kate. She'll be over the moon.'

'If I know my indomitable grandmother, she won't need telling. Like last time, when I confessed what I'd done—she'd known all along, and happily forgave me. Something else I don't deserve,' he added brokenly.

'And it's a criminal offence, kidnap,' Denise pointed out, attempting to ease the pain.

'But worth a life-sentence if I can spend it with you. You do love me, don't you?' he asked, suddenly unsure, the shadows in his eyes catching at her heart.

'Do you really need to ask?' she stalled. 'Oh, Adam, I hardly dare believe it. I'm so afraid I'm going to wake up and discover I've been dreaming. Only I'm not, am I? It's you and me for the rest of our lives. You, me—and our baby.'

'You and me forever,' he reassured her swiftly. Then, '*What* did you say?'

She laughed. The expression on his face was a curious mix of pride and sheer disbelief. 'Yes, my love,' she whispered, tears hovering on her lashes—tears of joy.

'But—how? When? Hell, Denise——' He ran his fingers through his hair, the dishevelled effect strangely appealing. 'Are you sure?'

'Oh, yes, I'm sure,' she reassured him simply. And she smiled inside as he snatched her close, cradling her head against his chest.

'I don't deserve this,' he murmured, burying his face in her hair, strong arms closing round, holding, enfolding, tenderly possessive. 'And to think I came so close to throwing it all away.'

'No, my love.' She raised her face to his, kissing away the pain. 'I walked out, I left you——'

'Hardly surprising in the circumstances. I should have explained, shouldn't I?' he asked. 'Jen, the hankie, the ball—I should have explained. Only, I didn't. I let pride come between us. But never again,' he vowed, hugging her fiercely. 'Never again—hey, my love?'

'Knowing you?' Denise laughed. 'Perhaps you'd better put it in writing.'

'I already have,' he told her throatily. 'It's part of the promise I made. To love and to cherish, from this day forward. Only, this time, we're both going to believe it.'

And then he kissed her, the past no longer important, the needs of the present banishing the shadows, their minds as one, bodies as one as the flames rekindled and the love of man and woman reaffirmed its faith. Love—honest, pure, undefiled and irreplaceably precious—driving the rest of the world far, far away.

Later she laughed, remembering Jen as she'd last seen her.

'Private joke?' he enquired, raising his head, his eyes gazing into hers and seeing to the centre of her soul.

'No, my love,' she told him huskily. 'No more secrets, no more pain. But if sir would care to ask me later, I've the most wonderful idea going through my mind.'

'So have I,' he growled delightedly, his hands beginning to roam her body in the most suggestive way. 'And judging from that look in your eyes, I do believe I'm going to enjoy each and every moment.' And then he kissed her, pausing for the briefest of moments to add softly, huskily, meaningfully, his heated glance a tangible caress, 'And so, my love, are you.'

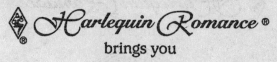

Harlequin Romance ®

brings you

How the West was Wooed!

We've rounded up twelve of our most popular authors, and the result is a whole year of romance, Western style. Every month we'll be bringing you a spirited, independent woman whose heart is about to be lassoed by a rugged, handsome, one-hundred-percent cowboy! Watch for...

- March: CLANTON'S WOMAN—Patricia Knoll

- April: A DANGEROUS MAGIC—Patricia Wilson

- May: THE BADLANDS BRIDE—Rebecca Winters

- June: RUNAWAY WEDDING—Ruth Jean Dale

- July: A RANCH, A RING AND EVERYTHING—Val Daniels

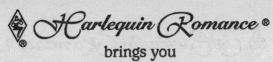

Harlequin Romance ®

brings you

HOLDING HERO ★ OUT FOR A

Some men are worth waiting for!

They're handsome, they're charming but, best of all, they're single! Twelve lucky women are about to discover that finding Mr. Right is not a problem—it's holding on to him.

In March the series continues with

#3401 THE ONLY MAN FOR MAGGIE
by Leigh Michaels

Karr Elliot wanted Maggie off his property but not out of his life. But Maggie didn't want a man—she wanted her own apartment!

Hold out for Harlequin Romance's heroes in coming months...

- April: THE RIGHT KIND OF MAN—Jessica Hart

- May: MOVING IN WITH ADAM—Jeanne Allan

- June: THE PARENT TRAP—Leigh Michaels

HOFH-3

UNLOCK THE DOOR TO GREAT ROMANCE
AT BRIDE'S BAY RESORT

Join Harlequin's new across-the-lines series, set
in an exclusive hotel on an island off the coast of
South Carolina.

Seven of your favorite authors will bring you exciting stories
about fascinating heroes and heroines discovering love at
Bride's Bay Resort.

Look for these fabulous stories coming to a store near you
beginning in January 1996.

Harlequin American Romance #613 in January
Matchmaking Baby by Cathy Gillen Thacker

Harlequin Presents #1794 in February
Indiscretions by Robyn Donald

Harlequin Intrigue #362 in March
Love and Lies by Dawn Stewardson

Harlequin Romance #3404 in April
Make Believe Engagement by Day Leclaire

Harlequin Temptation #588 in May
Stranger in the Night by Roseanne Williams

Harlequin Superromance #695 in June
Married to a Stranger by Connie Bennett

Harlequin Historicals #324 in July
Dulcie's Gift by Ruth Langan

Visit Bride's Bay Resort each month wherever
Harlequin books are sold.

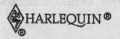

Harlequin Romance ®

New from Harlequin Romance
a very special six-book series by

MIDNIGHT SONS

DEBBIE MACOMBER

The town of Hard Luck, Alaska, needs women!

The O'Halloran brothers, who run a bush-plane service
called **Midnight Sons**, are heading a campaign to
attract women to Hard Luck. (*Location: north of the
Arctic Circle. Population: 150—mostly men!*)

"Debbie Macomber's *Midnight Sons* series is a delightful
romantic saga. And each book is a powerful, engaging story
in its own right. Unforgettable!"

—Linda Lael Miller

TITLE IN THE MIDNIGHT SONS SERIES:

Yo amo novelas con corazón!

Starting this March, Harlequin opens up to a whole new world of readers with two new romance lines in SPANISH!

Harlequin Deseo
- passionate, sensual and exciting stories

Harlequin Bianca
- romances that are fun, fresh and very contemporary

With four titles a month, each line will offer the same wonderfully romantic stories that you've come to love—now available in Spanish.

Look for them at selected retail outlets.

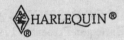 HARLEQUIN®

SPANT